WRITERS IN RESIDENCE

American Authors at Home

WRITERS IN RESIDENCE

American Authors at Home

Text and photographs by
Glynne Robinson Betts

With an Introduction by
Christopher Lehmann-Haupt

A Studio Book
The Viking Press
New York

For R.A.H.

First published in 1981 by
The Viking Press (A Studio Book)
625 Madison Avenue,
New York, N.Y. 10022
Published simultaneously in Canada
by Penguin Books Canada Limited

Library of Congress Cataloging in
Publication Data
Betts, Glynne.
   Writers in residence.
   (A Studio book)
   1. Authors, American—Homes and
haunts.   I. Title.
PS141.B4   810′.9 [B]   80-20887
ISBN 0-670-79108-3

Printed in the United States of
America
Set in Caledonia

Grateful acknowledgment is made to
the following for permission to reprint
copyrighted material from other
sources:

Dorothy Clausing: Portrait of Carl
Sandburg by Jan Clausing.

Harcourt Brace Jovanovich, Inc.: Two
lines from the poem "Prairie" from
Cornhuskers by Carl Sandburg.

Harper & Row, Publishers, Inc.: Text
excerpt from *Higglety Pigglety Pop!*
by Maurice Sendak. Courtesy of
Harper & Row, Publishers, Inc.

Mrs. Ellen C. Masters: Four lines
from "Petersburg" from *Illinois Poems*
by Edgar Lee Masters, Decker Press,
Prairie City, Illinois. Eighteen lines
from *Spoon River Anthology* by Edgar
Lee Masters, Macmillan.

North Carolina Department of
Cultural Resources: The photos taken
at the Thomas Wolfe Memorial, a
North Carolina State Historic Site,
appear here courtesy of the North
Carolina Department of Cultural
Resources.

Random House, Inc.: An excerpt from
"Tor House" from *Selected Poetry of
Robinson Jeffers.* Copyright 1928 and
renewed 1956 by Robinson Jeffers.

Mrs. Jill Faulkner Summers: Map
done by William Faulkner specifically
for *The Portable Faulkner.* Copyright
1946 by The Viking Press, Inc.
Copyright renewed 1974 by Viking
Penguin Inc.

Viking Penguin Inc.: Selections from
The Retrieval System by Maxine
Kumin. Copyright © 1975, 1976, 1977,
1978 by Maxine Kumin.

Acknowledgments

Many people—old friends and new—helped to make this book a reality. Among them are Jane Gordon at Orchard House; Ann Billesbach at the Willa Cather Pioneer Memorial; Professor Evans Harrington at the University of Mississippi; Helen Davis at the Zane Grey Museum; Mrs. Donnan C. Jeffers at Tor House; Dale Chodorow at Sunnyside; Melissa Brauer and Samuel S. Blane at the Petersburg Masters Museum; Betty and Clifford Bump of Lewistown, Illinois; Patricia Willis at the Rosenbach Foundation; Catherine Schmiesing at the Sinclair Lewis Foundation; Norma Millay Ellis and Ann-Ellen Lesser at the Millay Colony for the Arts; Mrs. Regina Cline O'Connor and Gerald Becham at the Georgia College Library, Milledgeville, Georgia; Katherine R. Hollander at the University of Maryland; Loraine Stevens at the Carl Sandburg Birthplace; Joseph Van Why at the Stowe-Day Foundation; Dexter Peck and Wynn Lee at Hartford's Mark Twain Memorial; Mimi and William Eric Williams; Steve Hill at the Thomas Wolfe Memorial; Eva Peterson and Carrie Martin at the Paul Laurence Dunbar House; and Kathleen McAuley at the Bronx Historical Society. I extend special thanks to my friends Graham Hatch, Natalie Robins, and Ginny McOmber, and to my family, whose help was indispensable, including my mother, Jessie M. Robinson, and my children, Liz, Will, and Kate Betts.

Both the selection of writers and any errors or omissions are my responsibility.

Contents

Preface

This book began in Asheville, North Carolina, a couple of years ago. The Asheville I expected to find was that of Thomas Wolfe and F. Scott Fitzgerald, a pretty southern town ringed by mountains, boasting fine old trees and two or three venerable hotels where people came to escape from the heat in the summer months or to restore their health in the good mountain air.

What I found was a small city ringed by mountains and highways, with a run-down center being urbanly renewed. The commercial activities of the town seemed to have moved to a strip of road lined with a McDonald's, a Holiday Inn, and the various components of a shopping plaza. Asheville was no different from hundreds of other American cities, I thought. In a last-ditch effort to find that romantic place fixed in my memory by the writings of Thomas Wolfe, I visited Dixieland.

Now a state-owned memorial, the house was called Old Kentucky Home when Wolfe's mother opened it as a boardinghouse in 1906. It was the writer's home for most of his youth, and he later immortalized it as Dixieland in his epic novel, *Look Homeward, Angel.* As I walked through the front door, I felt as if I had been carried back in time. I could see Eliza Gant's boarders rocking endlessly on the front porch in the afternoons and gathered in the parlor after supper; I could feel the frenzy of Eliza's activity in the kitchen, and I heard the clatter of china in the dining room. I took out my camera, photographed what I saw, and discovered back in New York that my pictures had actually captured a sense of the place. I had brought something home from Asheville, something of Thomas Wolfe and of Asheville as I had always known them in my mind's eye. Why couldn't I do that with other writers and their creative settings? So began this book.

We are all influenced by our environments, but writers' surroundings seem to shape their work as well as their lives. It is not coincidental that Frank Waters, author of *The Book of the Hopi,* has lived close to the Taos Pueblo for more than twenty-five years. Flannery O'Connor, William Faulkner, and Willa Cather were writers whose material was drawn from the regions of the country they knew best. Herman Melville was an exception. He had to move inland, away from the sea, before he could write *Moby Dick,* and scholars feel that the view of Mount Greylock from his study window in Pittsfield, Massachusetts, was his inspiration for the allegorical whale.

During the year that it took me to make the photographs for this book, I traveled all over America. The progression of my travels became important to some of the pictures. I could not approach Willa Cather's land by air; somehow it made a difference that I made the long trip to Nebraska by car. It was good to feel the country open up to the sky as I drove west, and the richness and fertility of the prairie Cather described so powerfully was all the more remarkable when approached from the flat plain of Kansas.

I wish I could describe my primordial feeling of well-being as I followed the Spoon River through lush Illinois farm country on a perfect summer day. I was looking for the best place to photograph that rural stream immortalized by Edgar Lee Masters, and those who knew Spoon River country best suggested that I go to a wide spot in the road called Bernadot. I rambled through fields that were alive with larks and blackbirds, the air fragrant with clover, winding up hill and down until I came to an ancient iron bridge over the placid river—and a dead end. A boy fishing on the riverbank said I was at Elrod.

I wasn't always alone in my search. You can imagine my surprise when I boarded the steamboat *Mark Twain* one evening in Hannibal, Missouri, for a twilight cruise on the Mississippi and found the same couple I had met in the graveyard commemorated by Masters at Lewistown, Illinois, three days earlier. They too were on a literary safari.

I won't soon forget that steamy bowl of homemade soup Annie Dillard had waiting when I arrived at her Connecticut home one fall afternoon just before a hurricane. Or the thump-thumping of Indian drums that broke the quiet as I tried to fall asleep in my motel room the night before my visit to Frank Waters in Taos. The concern of a curator in Indiana when she heard that I was traveling alone by car was not reassuring. "You'd better get yourself something," she cautioned. The "something" was a gun. The preparation of this book was my discovery of America.

Each writer's house that I visited brought a new sense of the writer and a new dimension to his work. The warmth and simplicity of Carl Sandburg's house moved me beyond words. I was touched by the tragic air that pervades the home of Paul Laurence Dunbar, who died after years of struggle at the peak of his career, aged 34; conversely, I was put off by the smugness reflected in the grandeur of Longfellow's house in Cambridge. Anaïs Nin's house in California was as distinctive as I expected it to be, and I could still sense the remoteness Robinson Jeffers felt when he began to build on a barren piece of California coastline in 1919, even though that point of land is now a fully developed residential area.

The writing room may be the most important room in the house to the writer, and its amenities can reveal much about the personallity of the individual. On separate coasts two distinguished women, Jessamyn West and Maxine Kumin, have carpeted and furnished hidden attic rooms where each goes to be by herself. William Faulkner's office was on the ground floor, overlooking his horses' paddock and stable. Marianne Moore had a chinning bar in the doorway near her desk, and when he lived in Hartford, Mark Twain wrote in the billiard room.

How did I choose the writers included in this book? That was easy. Most of them are drawn from my lifetime list of personal favorites, and when I see them together now I realize that they reflect a wide variety of personalities and ways of living that is particularly American.

A sense of place, a sense of *the* place, is what I have tried to convey in my photographs. Each situation was different, and the approach to each was dictated by the circumstance of my visit, the mood of the day, the weather, the people, and the place itself.

This book, then, started as a journal of personal impressions both photographic and verbal, but as it went along it took on a distinct shape, resulting in a visual record of the life-styles and individuality of some people who write.

Introduction

by Christopher Lehmann-Haupt

When Glynne Robinson Betts first told me about her plans for the book *Writers in Residence*, I thought: Of course, a book about place; all writers need a sense of place to get their words on paper. I didn't mean a place to write *about* so much as a place to write *in*, though obviously, as the following pages remind us, William Faulkner and Sinclair Lewis would not have achieved what they did without Lafayette County, Mississippi, and Sauk Centre, Minnesota, to transform into Yoknapatawpha and Gopher Prairie. All writers come from someplace, and that someplace tends to haunt their imaginations, even if it gets transfigured into as fantastic a world as Samuel Butler's Erewhon or Vladimir Nabokov's Antiterra.

I've often wondered how important such a sense of place is to the business of putting words on paper. Anyone who has tried to commit even so humble an act of prose as an outraged letter to the electric utility knows that the environment for writing is never perfect. If only your chair were a little lower, or your desk a little higher. If only there weren't so many interesting objects in sight. If only your neighbor would turn down his stereo so you could hear the peaceful sounds of nature. If only the birds would stop twittering. If only there weren't so many things to do besides write. If only your pencils were a little sharper.

While sharpening my pencils, I think of the extremes to which some writers have gone in order to create a sense of place to work in. I think of the famous writer who used to reach his office by walking a six-by-one-foot wooden plank suspended twenty feet in the air, which he hoped would separate his workplace from the rest of the household—until his children began to use the plank as a jungle gym. I think of another writer who, after packing her family off to work and school in the morning, used to leave her Greenwich Village brownstone, walk once around the block, enter her front door, and—taking great care not to look at the dust on the carpet or the dishes in the sink—march straight upstairs and lock herself in her office. I think of Marcel Proust in his famous cork-lined cell.

Of course, such rituals and extremes seem slightly laughable when you think of Oscar Wilde or Jean Genet turning out their books in prison—although, come to think of it, maybe prison is an ideal place to write. What, after all, is the difference between jail and a writers' colony except that you can leave a writers' colony, provided your conscience allows. When writers complain about the difficulty of finding a quiet place to work, I can't help thinking of Karl Marx, who is supposed to have written difficult passages of *Das Kapital* while playing horsie with his children in the squalor of his London flat. Or of the many newspaper reviewers I have watched bang out their prose while the chaos of the newsroom swirled around them. But then Marx was only exercising his powers of reason, considerable though they were, which is easy compared with writing a poem, play, or novel. And the newspapermen were working against deadlines, which—as Samuel Johnson pointed out apropos of hanging—possess a singular power to concentrate the mind.

Glynne Robinson Betts, in her photographic odyssey, has revealed some of the secrets of how writers create that magic sense of place, although a first glance at these pages might seem inconclusive. Depicted in what follows is an absolute cornucopia of discomfort and clutter. Just imagine trying to write on that tiny table in Louisa May Alcott's bedroom. And how Samuel Clemens became Mark Twain with the temptation of a billiard table before his eyes surpasses my understanding. Yet the record is certain that the hours spent in these spaces have been fruitful. Why, many of the writers in these pages even look happy—although it should probably be noted that very few of them are actually writing. They have written, which is one of the most blissful states known to humanity. Or they are preparing to write, which is not so benign a condition, but still tolerable. But none of them is really at it, except Malcolm Cowley, Margaret Millar, and May Sarton, and from their looks of tranquility one would have to guess they are posing. Indeed, I wonder if any writer has ever been photographed in the true act of writing. I tend to doubt it. It would not be a pretty picture.

But if a glance at these pages proves inconclusive, a closer look can teach us something about the way good writers work. Take the matter of the visual environment—what a writer looks at while working, or, more precisely, what he looks at while leaning back in his chair, trying to decide what to write next. I've always wondered whether it's better to have a blank space around you—the visual counterpart of Proust's cork-lined room—so that everything which comes to mind springs directly from the imagination, so to speak. Or is it preferable to be surrounded by objects on which to fasten the eyes occasionally? Obviously, if you've been seized by a powerful vision you're not going to be distracted by what you see in front of you. A writer working full steam ahead goes into a kind of trance; I don't imagine William Faulkner would have allowed one of those sentences to be interrupted even in the unlikely event that an automobile accident occurred outside his window. That is why, I suspect, so many writers represented in these pages could afford to work amid such clutter. Anyway—as anyone who has ever tried to remind himself to pay a bill he doesn't want to pay by placing

it in a prominent place on his desk will have noticed—objects have a way of becoming so familiar that they cease to exist after a while.

Still, even the most possessed of us comes out of the trance every now and then. Does it matter what there is for us to see when we do? Evidently it does, to judge from Glynne Betts's photographs. Both Maxine Kumin and Annie Dillard have little clusters of photographs and paintings to look at when they run out of fuel. Many others have the views outside their windows, although it should be noted that Flannery O'Connor kept her desk turned *away* from her workroom window's inviting view. And on a clear day Herman Melville could see his leviathan from his farmhouse in the Berkshires. For as Glynne Betts confirms, "Mount Greylock does look like a whale surfacing on the northern horizon." Melville's example seems to clinch the case for the role of the visual environment in writing. Whether or not he really visualized Mount Greylock as Moby Dick, he evidently did see his house and its surroundings as a ship at sea. Thus it served as both a stimulus to memory and a retreat from the hurly-burly —in short, the ideal place for a writer to reside.

But the most important secret that Glynne Betts has revealed in these pages can only be discovered by reading the graceful essays she provides to illuminate her photographs. Again and again in these commentaries we come upon descriptions of the hours the various writers keep. And almost invariably they seem to prefer working in the morning and quitting fairly early in the day. Herman Melville would stop at two-thirty when, as he wrote a friend, "I hear a preconcerted knock at my door, which serves to wean me effectively from my writing, however interested I may be." Scott and Helen Nearing start receiving guests at three in the afternoon. May Sarton quits at noon. William Faulkner called it a day by ten-thirty or eleven. Flannery O'Connor and Robinson

Jeffers wrote only in the morning. Carl Sandburg alone departs from the pattern of the writers here who report their habits, and he stopped earliest of all, because he wrote through the night and quit in time for milking.

A pretty good way to make a living, you might think—to be free to frolic away the afternoons of your life. But you mustn't be fooled. Anyone who has ever tried to write knows that you don't just sit down and bang it out. It is necessary first to seethe and torment yourself. Robert Frost may have written many of his poems at single sittings, as he boasted, but weeks of reflection, if not a lifetime, went into them first. An idea must have a chance to work its way out of the brain and into the viscera before it goes down on the page. How do good writers help this process along? I'm delighted to see that Glynne Betts has provided one answer. Good writers work themselves physically. Melville and Sandburg did farm chores. H. L. Mencken, William Carlos Williams, and Edna St. Vincent Millay all gardened. Malcolm Cowley saws wood. And Robinson Jeffers did stonework as a daily ritual, adding one room after another to the house he had built himself in Carmel, California, with huge stones he hauled up from the beach below. I like the image that routine suggests—Jeffers struggling to catch flighty words in the morning and lifting heavy stones in the afternoon. It's as if the one activity gave substance and form to the other.

"The best place for a writer to work is in his head," Malcolm Cowley says in these pages, attributing the remark to Ernest Hemingway. Cowley and Hemingway are right, but the head must be someplace for the writer to work well in it. In the pages that follow, Glynne Robinson Betts has given us more than rooms and views and houses. She has shown us many places where good work has been done.

Bronson Alcott & Louisa May Alcott

> *"It was a comfortable old room, though the carpet was faded and the furniture very plain; for a good picture or two hung on the walls, books filled the recesses, chrysanthemums and Christmas roses bloomed in the windows, and a pleasant atmosphere of home-peace pervaded it."*
>
> —Little Women

What would people today think of someone who sat under a tree in front of his house, waiting to engage passersby in philosophical discussions? Eccentric, to say the least. But the citizens of Concord, Massachusetts, in the mid-nineteenth century, saw nothing unusual in Amos Bronson Alcott's behavior. After all, they were used to such unconventional neighbors as Nathaniel Hawthorne, Ralph Waldo Emerson, and Henry David Thoreau.

Bronson Alcott's individualism is representative of the Transcendentalists, that unusual group of writers in Concord who believed in the unity of all things and the divinity of man. "Trust thyself," Emerson's motto, became their watchword. Alcott called the town Concordia and settled his family there after the failure of his experimental Temple School in Boston and his communal farm at Fruitlands, near Harvard, Massachusetts. He believed that his thoughts and conversation were a highly prized resource and that it was his wife's duty to support the family—a responsibility later assumed by his daughter Louisa May. Meanwhile, Bronson Alcott was free to write in his journal, work on his book *Concord Days,* and expound his radical theories of education to anyone who was interested.

Photo of Bronson Alcott courtesy Concord Free Public Library.

Orchard House became the Alcott family's permanent home. The two-storied clapboard house, which sits on a slope overlooking the Lexington Road, was a dilapidated farmhouse on ten acres with an apple orchard of forty trees when the family moved there in 1858. It has small windows, low ceilings, and undersized rooms with uneven plank floors. Bronson Alcott constructed bookcases, made wall alcoves for the classical busts he had brought from his Temple School, and dug a vegetable garden to feed the family through the year.

Alcott's study was just inside the front door across from the family parlor. It was filled with books, and had arches and classical pillars befitting the tastes of an idealistic philosopher. Bronson Alcott was visited here almost daily by his good friend Ralph Waldo Emerson. The two men held long philosophical discussions, each considering the other the ideal intellectual companion.

Bronson Alcott's intense second daughter, Louisa May, realized early in life that she would be forced by their indigence to assume her mother's role as the family's sole provider. She worked hard in Boston teaching and then writing to support her parents and two surviving sisters, but returned to Orchard House at the age of thirty-five to write *Little Women,* her most popular book, which was based on her own family's experiences.

Louisa May Alcott did her writing at a small table beneath the window in her sunny upstairs bedroom at Orchard House. She worked long hours every day, pulling a shawl around her shoulders when the old house became too drafty.

After Louisa became famous, Bronson would describe

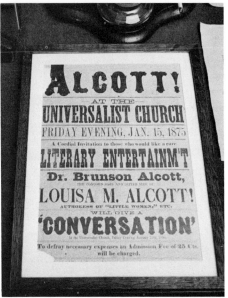

Orchard House, the Alcott family home in Concord, Massachusetts.
"They always looked back before turning the corner, for their mother was always at the window, to nod and smile, and wave her hand to them."

—Little Women

A philosopher is "a man up in a balloon, with his family and friends holding the ropes which confine him to earth," Louisa May Alcott wrote in her journal after the opening of her father's School of Philosophy in 1879.

her in his public "conversations" as an example of the ideal woman, one whose character had been developed along the lines he had prescribed. Louisa seems to have resented this as well as her father's otherworldly ways. When his School of Philosophy opened in 1879 for its second summer session at their house, she wrote in her journal that she was angered by the philosophers who "roost on our steps like hens waiting for corn. Father revels in it so we keep the hotel going and try to look as if we liked it."

Amos Bronson Alcott (1799–1888)—b. near Wolcott, Connecticut.
Major works: *Tablets, Observations on the Principles and Methods of Infant Instruction, Orphic Sayings.*

Louisa May Alcott (1832–1888)—b. Germantown, Pennsylvania.
Major works: *Little Women, An Old-Fashioned Girl, Little Men, Eight Cousins, Rose in Bloom, Under the Lilacs.*

The Orchard House, Lexington Road, Concord, Massachusetts, open to the public.

*This 1871 portrait
of Louisa May
by George Healy
hangs in the
Orchard House
dining room.*

*Above Louisa May's writing table in a
sunny corner of her bedroom hangs a
portrait of her niece and namesake, Lulu,
the daughter of her younger sister May.*

"The dim, dusty room, with the busts staring down from the tall bookcases, the cosy chairs, the globes, and, best of all, the wilderness of books . . . made the library a region of bliss to her," Louisa May wrote in Little Women, *describing her father's study. Bronson Alcott always carried a small bust of Socrates in his pocket. When he was "at home" for his family, he placed the statue on the study mantelpiece.*

Henry Wadsworth Longfellow

"*We have purchased an old mansion here, built before the revolution and occupied by Washington as his headquarters when the American army was in Cambridge. It is a fine old house, and I have a strong attachment from having lived in it since I first came to Cambridge . . . in the rear I yesterday planted an avenue of Linden trees, which already begin to be ten or twelve feet high. I have also planted some acorns, and as the oak grows for a thousand years, you may imagine a whole line of little Longfellows, like the shadowy monarchs in Macbeth walking under their branches, through countless generations . . . all blessing the man who planted them (meaning, the oaks).*"

—*From a letter, 1843*

Henry Wadsworth Longfellow, painted by his son Ernest, 1876.

How could the author of *Hiawatha* and "The Village Blacksmith" live in such a grand manner, I wondered on entering Henry Wadsworth Longfellow's house in Cambridge, Massachusetts. This was the poet's home for forty-five years and it is filled with antiques, paintings, and decorative objects of the period, unlike any other professor-poet's house I had ever seen.

Longfellow first lived in the house as a boarder of Mrs. Craigie, a widow, after he moved from Maine to be professor of modern languages at Harvard. When he married Frances Appleton in 1843, her rich father purchased the house for the couple as a wedding present and it remained the poet's home for the rest of his life.

The Longfellow House is rich in history. General George Washington lived there in 1775 when he took command of the Continental Army at the beginning of the Revolution. His office was the room that Longfellow later used as a study.

This study is crowded with mementos of his literary career and his friendships, and is supposed to be just as the poet left it when he died; even the buff-brown walls and "turkey-red" draperies are unchanged. He worked at the round table in the center of the room, using a folding lap desk at which he wrote most of his poems, including "The Children's Hour," where he described how his three young daughters would slip into the room and climb over the arms and back of his chair while he was writing.

Henry Wadsworth Longfellow was not like most poets. He was a national institution. Extraordinarily popular as a romantic who idealized his subjects, he created a new audience for poetry in America and abroad. Ten thousand copies of *The Courtship of Miles Standish* sold in London in one day.

Henry Wadsworth Longfellow (1807–1882)—b. Portland, Maine. **Major works:** *Voices of the Night, Evangeline, Hiawatha, The Courtship of Miles Standish, Tales of a Wayside Inn, Kavanagh, Christus.*

The Longfellow House, 105 Brattle Street, Cambridge, Massachusetts, open to the public.

*The Longfellow
house on
Brattle Street
in Cambridge
was built
in 1759.*

*The standing desk
offered Longfellow
a view across fields
to the Charles River.*

The ebonized armchair (right) was made of wood from the "spreading chestnut tree" and presented to the poet on his seventy-second birthday by the schoolchildren of Cambridge. A copy of Jean Antoine Houdon's bust of Washington greets visitors in the front hall of the Longfellow house (above). The large painting of a woman by Washington Allston belonged to Mrs. Longfellow's family.

"I love best to think of him in his study, where he
wrought at his lovely art with a serenity expressed in
his smooth, regular, and scrupulously perfect
handwriting. . . . Each letter was distinct in shape and
between the verses was always the exact space of
half an inch. . . . I once asked him if he were not a
great deal interrupted, and he said, with a faint sigh,
not more than was good for him, he fancied; if it
were not for the interruptions, he might overwork."

—*William Dean Howells,*
Literary Friends and Acquaintances, *1901*

Harriet Beecher Stowe

> **"** *It has been shown that the best end for a woman to seek is the training of God's children for their eternal home, by guiding them to intelligence, virtue, and true happiness. When, therefore, the wise woman seeks a home in which to exercise this ministry, she will aim to secure a house so planned that it will provide in the best manner for health, industry, and economy, those cardinal requisites of domestic enjoyment and success.* **"**
>
> —The American Woman's Home

I discovered Harriet Beecher Stowe, the dynamic daughter of the Puritan ethic, in Hartford, Connecticut, and have felt humble ever since. She was the wonder woman of her time, and in her Hartford house reminders of her energy are everywhere.

When not ministering to the whims of her temperamental husband, Professor Calvin Stowe, she supervised a large household, wrote several books, stenciled furniture, and painted in oil with a highly individual style. And all this was after the age of sixty. Her success as an author and crusader had preceded this second burst of energy.

As young Harriet Beecher she had lived happily in Hartford, after spending seven years there as a student and then as a teacher, in her sister Catherine's Hartford Female Seminary. She vowed to return there to live someday. During the intervening years she lived in Cincinnati, where she was involved with the abolitionist movement, wrote tracts, and married Professor Stowe, a prominent theologian. She raised a family of five children, became a fiction writer of some note, and wrote *Uncle Tom's Cabin,* an incredibly popular novel that caused Americans to take a more careful look at the evils of slavery.

Photo of Harriet Beecher Stowe in her front parlor, c. 1886, courtesy Stowe-Day Foundation.

When Calvin Stowe retired from teaching at the Theological Seminary at Andover, Massachusetts, the Stowes moved to Hartford. Now internationally famous as a crusading writer, Harriet Beecher Stowe turned to homelier subject matter such as family life in New England, home economics, and interior decoration.

I found the house anything but the dark and forbidding Victorian "cottage" it seems from the outside. It is a warm family home filled with the signs and clutter of a long, productive life.

The downstairs rooms in the twelve-room house are striking reminders of Mrs. Stowe's creative versatility. Her paintings adorn the walls, and many innovative furnishings and decorating ideas of the writer are employed throughout.

Harriet Beecher Stowe's second-floor study was, for me, the most compelling room in the house. A tiny closet of a room compared to the others, it was next to her bedroom and had one window. Five books were written here on furniture that was entirely hand-painted by the author.

Harriet Beecher Stowe (1811–1896)—b. Litchfield, Connecticut.
Major works: *Uncle Tom's Cabin, The Minister's Wooing, The Pearl of Orr's Island, Oldtown Folks, The American Woman's Home, Lady Byron Vindicated, Our Famous Women.*

The Harriet Beecher Stowe House, the Stowe-Day Foundation, 77 Forest Street, Hartford, Connecticut, open to the public.

The Stowes' substantial house at Nook Farm, Hartford's literary neighborhood at the end of the nineteenth century.

"The use of ivy in decorating a room is beginning to be generally acknowledged," Mrs. Stowe wrote in 1869 in The American Woman's Home, *of which she was co-author with her sister Catherine Beecher and which became the housewife's bible of the late nineteenth century. She obviously practiced what she preached.*

The author of Uncle Tom's Cabin *played Negro spirituals and hymns at this piano, watched over by a portrait of her husband Calvin's first wife, Eliza.*

A portrait of Henry Ward Beecher, her favorite brother, hangs over the mantel in the front parlor in the house at Nook Farm. He was a famous minister who discussed every important issue of the day from his Brooklyn pulpit and was an eloquent spokesman for the abolitionist cause.

"If parents wish their daughters to grow up with good domestic habits, they should have, as one means of securing this result, a neat and cheerful kitchen," Mrs. Stowe wrote. Her own kitchen was a model of the advanced ideas introduced in her book, including storage bins and an unusual stove. The workroom (opposite) where Mrs. Stowe wrote Poganuc People, a novel of New England based on her childhood in Litchfield, Connecticut, contains furniture painted by the writer herself.

Herman Melville

" *. . . at nights when I wake up and hear the wind shrieking, I almost fancy there is too much sail on the house, & I had better go on the roof and rig in the chimney.* **"**

—From a letter, 1850

Photo of Herman Melville, 1885, courtesy Gansevoort-Lansing Collection, New York Public Library.

*M*ount Greylock *does* look like a whale surfacing on the northern horizon, and the long, wooden porch at Arrowhead Farm, which Herman Melville called the "Piazza," could be the deck of a ship. In a letter Melville wrote, he said, "I have a sort of sea-feeling here in the country, now that the ground is all covered with snow. I look out of my window in the morning when I rise as I would out of a porthole of a ship in the Atlantic." For Melville, the loneliness of this remote farm in the Berkshires must have been familiar after his years at sea, and it is not difficult to understand how the allegorical *Moby Dick* was written here.

Melville moved his family to the farm in 1850 from New York and, during his fourteen years there, balanced his time spent writing with heavy farm labor, growing the family's food, keeping livestock, and patching the old buildings around the place. "Since you have been here . . . I have been plowing and sowing and raising and painting and printing and praying," he wrote to Nathaniel Hawthorne, his close friend in neighboring Lenox. The two writers often took long hikes together around the countryside and during the winter they would hold long, intense discussions in Melville's barn.

The writer's study was on the second floor of the simple frame farmhouse and looked out on Mount Greylock, a few miles to the north. Melville once described his writing habits in a letter to a friend: "My own breakfast over, I go to my workroom & light my fire—then spread my M.S.S. on the table—take one business squint at it, & fall to with a will. At 2½ P.M. I hear a preconcerted knock at my door, which serves to wean me effectively from my writing, however interested I may be. My friends the horse & cow now demand their dinner."

I could not help reflecting on the power of Herman Melville's imagination when I visited his landlocked farm, one hundred fifty miles from the sea, on an unusually clear August afternoon. Mount Greylock loomed blue in the distance, a permanent guardian of the spirit of this brooding man.

Herman Melville (1819–1891)—b. New York City, New York.
Major works: *Typee: A Peep at Polynesian Life, Mardi, Redburn, Moby Dick, The Piazza Tales.*

Arrowhead, 780 Holmes Road, Pittsfield, Massachusetts, open to the public.

"I rise at eight—thereabouts—& go to my barn—Say good morning to the horse, & give him his breakfast. (It goes to my heart to give him a cold one, but it can't be helped.)"

—From a letter, 1850

Quotations from Melville's essay "I and My Chimney" are still visible on the brick fireplace at Arrowhead.

"You and I—must hit upon some little bit of vagabondism, before Autumn comes. Greylock—we must go and vagabondize there," Melville wrote to Nathaniel Hawthorne in nearby Lenox, Massachusetts, in 1851.

Mark Twain

" *My billiard table is stacked up with books relating to the Sandwich Islands: the walls are upholstered with scraps of paper penciled with notes drawn from them. I have saturated myself with knowledge of that unimaginably beautiful land and that most strange and fascinating people. And I have begun a story.* **"**

—From a letter to William Dean Howells, 1884

Drawing of Mark Twain by Arthur Jule Goodman, 1891, courtesy New York Public Library.

In 1874 the *Hartford Daily Times* called this house "one of the oddest looking buildings in the state," but of the many places he lived in during his lifetime, "home" for Mark Twain was always the unique dwelling he built for his family on Nook Farm in Hartford, Connecticut.

Nook Farm was the literary neighborhood of that period. Harriet Beecher Stowe lived next door, Charles Dudley Warner nearby. Critic William Dean Howells noted that Twain built "the stately mansion in which he satisfied his love of magnificence as if it had been another sealskin coat." Every detail was considered and no expense spared in the construction of the house, which had decks, carved railings, and other features of a Mississippi steamboat, including a tower that resembles a wheelhouse. Here the writer and his family lived for seventeen years until the death of his daughter Susy and badly managed finances forced Mark Twain to sell.

When I visited the Hartford house, it was easy to see how Mark Twain's money just seemed to evaporate in keeping up his lavish life-style. The nineteen-room house was adorned with the most elegant furnishings of the period; the front hall itself had been designed and decorated by Louis Comfort Tiffany.

Mark Twain loved to entertain, and there was a constant stream of daily visitors and house guests.

In a letter from London Mark Twain wrote, "To us, our house was not unsentient matter—it had a heart, and a soul, and eyes to see us with; and approvals, and solicitudes, and deep sympathies; it was of us, and we were in its confidence, and lived in its grace and in the peace of its benediction. We never came home from an absence that its face did not light up and speak out its eloquent welcome— and we could not enter it unmoved."

Mark Twain (1835–1910)—b. Samuel Langhorne Clemens, Florida, Missouri.
Major works: *The Innocents Abroad, The Prince and the Pauper, Life on the Mississippi, The Adventures of Tom Sawyer, The Adventures of Huckleberry Finn, A Connecticut Yankee in King Arthur's Court.*

The Mark Twain Memorial, 351 Farmington Avenue, Hartford, Connecticut, open to the public. Mark Twain's Boyhood Home, 208 Hill Street, Hannibal, Missouri, open to the public.

Hannibal, Missouri, was Mark Twain's childhood home but only one of more than a dozen places in which he lived during his peripatetic life.

The Clemens family house in Hartford (top) has decks and other design features strikingly similar to those of Twain's beloved Mississippi riverboats (opposite right), even a balcony that looks like a wheelhouse. Mrs. Clemens and her three daughters are pictured on the porch of the house (opposite left). (Courtesy New York Public Library.)

"Clemens had appointed himself, with the architect's connivance, a luxurious study over the library in his new house, but as his children grew older this study, with its carved and cushioned armchairs, was given over to them for a schoolroom. . . ."

"He discovered that he could make a more commodious use of the billiard-room at the top of his house, for the purposes of literature and friendship. . . . We had a peculiar pleasure in looking off from the high windows on the pretty Hartford landscape, and down from them into the tops of the trees clothing the hillside by which his house stood. We agreed that there was a novel charm in trees seen from such a vantage, far surpassing that of the farther scenery. He had not been a country boy for nothing."

—William Dean Howells, Literary Friends and Acquaintances, *1901*

Edith Wharton

> **"***The Mount was to give me country cares and joys, long happy rides and drives through the wooded lanes of that loveliest region, the companionship of a few dear friends, and the freedom from trivial obligations which was necessary if I was to go on with my writing. The Mount was my first real home.***"**

—A Backward Glance

Photo of Edith Wharton, c. 1908, courtesy Collection of American Literature, Beinecke Rare Book and Manuscript Library, Yale University.

A few miles down the road from Herman Melville's modest farmhouse in the Berkshires, but a world away, is the Mount, the summer home of Edith Wharton. Through the hedge I had a glimpse of the grandeur of a bygone age.

Edith Wharton and her husband built the Mount at the turn of the century to escape from Newport and the "watering-place trivialities. . . . If I could have made the change sooner I daresay I should never have given a thought to the literary delights of Paris or London." It was their summer retreat for ten years, until the drastic decline of her husband's health made the burden of the estate too great for Mrs. Wharton and she moved permanently to Europe. "The country quiet stimulated my creative zeal," she wrote later of her years in the Berkshires.

The Mount, which resembles a French château, was composed of extensive gardens, a farm, and woodlands. Life there was an extravagant blend of simple country pleasures and sophisticated conversation. Henry James made frequent and lengthy visits. His "curious inadaptability," as Mrs. Wharton put it, to the summer heat was relieved only by "incessant motoring" around the Massachusetts countryside in the Whartons' grand automobile. Long summer evenings were passed in conversation on the "dear, wide" terrace of the Mount, which is now the summer home of a Shakespearean theater company.

Edith Wharton (1862–1937)—b. New York City, New York.
Major works: *The Valley of Decision, The House of Mirth, Ethan Frome, Summer, The Age of Innocence* (1920 Pulitzer Prize), *Xingu and Other Stories.*

The Mount, Lenox, Massachusetts, not open to the public.

Helen & Scott Nearing

"We choose to live quietly and simply, to exercise in the open air, to keep sensible hours and not overdo physically. We choose to exercise our bodies not in gymnasiums or on golf courses or tennis courts but doing useful outdoor physical work. We choose to live in the country rather than the city, with its polluted air, noise, and stress. We prefer clean fresh air, sunshine, clear running water. We choose to cut our own fuel in our woods rather than pay the oil barons. We design and construct our own buildings. We grow and prepare our own food, rather than shop in supermarkets."

—Continuing the Good Life

What did we do before the camera was invented?" asked Scott Nearing as he looked down the lens of my Nikon while preparing to saw a monstrous log for firewood.

"Well, the camera has been around for a long time," I replied.

"How long?" he asked.

"Oh, more than a hundred years."

"It all depends on your perspective!" said the ninety-seven-year-old Nearing with a twinkle.

Scott Nearing left mainstream America and began to live what he calls "the good life" more than fifty years ago, and he has been writing about it ever since. Scott and his wife, Helen, vigorous advocates of organic gardening and subsistence living, feel that their style of life enables them to "live harmlessly in a violent world."

When the area around their first homestead in Vermont began to develop as a popular ski resort, the Nearings pulled up stakes and moved to a remote farm in Maine. That was twenty years ago. Since then, with their own hands, they have built fourteen structures of stone there, including a spacious two-storied house. When their daily round of outdoor chores are finished, they retire to the house to write.

Helen works on current writing projects at a refectory table near the huge living-room window overlooking Penobscot Bay. Scott prefers to write at a card table in his small bedroom under the eaves. This combination of physical labor and creative intellectual activity, which includes a regular stint on the lecture circuit, presents such an enviable life-style that the Nearings have been overwhelmed with visitors, finding it necessary to post visiting hours on a rock in their driveway.

Scott Nearing (1883–)—b. Morris Run, Pennsylvania.
Helen Nearing (1904–)—b. Ridgewood, New Jersey.
Major works: By Scott Nearing: *The Conscience of a Radical, The Making of a Radical.* By Helen and Scott Nearing: *The Maple Sugar Book, Living the Good Life, Continuing the Good Life.*

They live in Harborside, Deer Isle, Maine.

Our Mornings are Our Own
We'll see Visitors 3-5
Help us live the GOOD LIFE
Helen & Scott.

"Helen designed the house to fit into the landscape. She wanted an alpine-type building with a broad sloping roof."

"The first finished project on the new place was a stone and concrete outhouse. . . ."

—Continuing the Good Life

Herbs hung from the ceiling beams and the wood cooking stove are the only old-fashioned features in the otherwise modern kitchen of the Nearings' farmhouse. Wood for the winter, sorted and stored according to size and use, reveals their systematic approach to living on the land.

"There are many things we enjoy doing about the place. . . . Give us a good-size job of building with stone and concrete, with time and materials to do the work well. Now that the house is built, and we are living in and enjoying it, we look around us at piles of rocks still unused and wonder: What next?"

—Continuing the Good Life

Malcolm Cowley

"*In the end, after starting with goodwill and $300, I was to find myself possessed of, or by, a seven-room house, a cornfield, a briar patch, a trout brook, and a crazy edifice of debts to be razed stone by stone.***"**

—The Dream of the Golden Mountains

The best place for a writer to work is in his head." Malcolm Cowley attributes the remark to Ernest Hemingway and notes that after this essential fact has been established, the variety of writers' work habits is as great as the number of writers. He should know. As critic and poet, Cowley has had his finger on America's literary pulse for more than fifty years, and no one has written more gracefully or lovingly about the craft of writing in this century. It was Malcolm Cowley who brought the work of William Faulkner to national prominence when he edited *The Portable Faulkner* in 1945.

Cowley moved his family to rural Connecticut from New York City in the late 1930s, when land there was inexpensive and the living was easier. The Cowleys made their charming house from an old barn on the property, dug a garden behind it, and then planted a huge pine forest behind the garden. The flavor of those earlier days is recalled in a letter that Cowley wrote to William Faulkner: "I have a pheasant-feeding station outside my study window. I watch them when I ought to be writing. . . . One cock roosts in my pine trees at night. . . . When I come out to saw wood just before sunset he raises a hell of a racket. 'These are my trees,' he seems to be saying."

Malcolm Cowley works upstairs in a dormered, white-walled study under the eaves. Crowded with books and files, the small room is furnished with a utilitarian gray steel desk and a unique typewriter-table arrangement that, despite the writer's assurances to the contrary, looks desperately uncomfortable. With his legs crammed under the small steel table, and his feet propped on a specially made wooden platform that keeps the table from skidding around the room as he pounds the keys of the typewriter, Malcolm Cowley writes.

Malcolm Cowley (1898–   )—b. near Belsano, Pennsylvania.
Major works: *Exile's Return, After the Genteel Tradition, The Literary Situation, The Faulkner–Cowley File, Blue Juniata, Think Back on Us, Collected Poems, A Second Flowering: Works and Days of the Lost Generation, —And I Worked at the Writer's Trade, The Dream of the Golden Mountains.*

He lives in Sherman, Connecticut.

*Portrait of the author
at forty, painted
by his friend and
neighbor Alexander
Calder.*

May Sarton

" *. . . One does not need to show off a house, only live in it, to make a true shelter and nurturing place for human needs . . . a cat sitting on a table to look out, a bowl of flowering bulbs, books scattered about.* **""**

—Journal of a Solitude

*Y*ou are late," said May Sarton in a rich, theatrical voice as she opened the door of her sun-filled cottage on the Maine coast. I had lost my way. She looked as though I had ruined her day.

"I'll leave then," I said.

"No, come in. You've driven such a long way. What would you like to photograph first?" she asked brusquely.

We climbed three flights of stairs to her study. She sat down at the desk surrounded by pictures—photos of Lotte Jacobi, Colette, and other friends—and drew my attention to the difficult backlight situation caused by the dark, paneled walls. Suddenly, the mood of our meeting shifted to one of lightness and friendship.

May Sarton, who lives alone, moved to her Maine house from New Hampshire several years ago, at the invitation of friends who had bought it as part of an estate and built a modern house for themselves nearby. She wrote in her *Journal of a Solitude:*

"I saw it yesterday, and am imagining myself into it, feeling a little clumsy . . . built in the 1920s, is

my guess, solid and comfortable, with a superb outlook right down a golden meadow to the ocean itself. I roved about it trying to find a nest where I could work, and it is just that that I wonder about. But I have an idea that a rather sheltering paneled room on the third floor might work. And oh, the sea—."

The house, painted bright yellow, is surrounded by gardens and flowering shrubs. An insatiable gardener, May Sarton showed me her prized clematis and a stunning border of scarlet and yellow tuberous begonias. There are flowering houseplants and bouquets in almost every

room of the house, and she delights in the greenhouse effect she has created with a bay window.

Sarton is an early riser and spends mornings at work in her study, breaking at midday to take a long walk and collect her mail. The poet and novelist thinks of herself as a poet first because she feels poetry is "so much more a true work of the soul than prose." Her subjects for novels are often less popular concerns—old age, lesbianism, cancer—brilliantly articulated in prose, and she is surprised by the popularity of her *Journal of a Solitude* among college students. May Sarton cautions them to immerse themselves fully in life, and thereby to grow.

May Sarton (1912–   )—b. Wondelgem, Belgium.
Major works: Poetry: *Inner Landscape, A Private Mythology, A Grain of Mustard Seed.* Novels: *The Small Room, Mrs. Stevens Hears the Mermaids Singing, As We Are Now.* Nonfiction: *I Knew a Phoenix, Journal of a Solitude, Recovering.*

She lives in York, Maine.

"The clematis along the fence has never been so beautiful, starry hosts, white, purple, a strange pale pink; one is almost true blue, one very dark purple, almost black."

—The House by the Sea

"Here on the third floor I look about me and feel extremely happy. This is a beautiful place to work, the wood paneling such a soft brown. But the great thing is that being so high up (for the house stands on a knoll) I am in the treetops on two sides, and on the third, where I sit, I look out over the field to open sea."

—The House by the Sea

"Birds are an important part of my life here, especially in winter. The feeders are outside the closed-in porch where I have my meals, read, and look at TV when I am downstairs. Lately a flock of evening grosbeaks comes and goes among the chickadees, three sparrows, and goldfinches."

—The House by the Sea

Maxine Kumin

> *The first sound Robin heard the day she came back alone to Little Mink Hill was the bleating of the vealers. A pair of swallows had nested in New Jersey's lean-to. Chipmunks were busy in what remained of last winter's woodpile. She dawdled there, floating, her bones grown light as milkweed puffs as in a sudden moment of* déjà vu.

—The Designated Heir

October was nearly over, and Maxine Kumin was getting ready for winter. As I drove up the steep driveway to her red clapboard farmhouse in New Hampshire, the shrill sound of a chain saw pierced the country quiet. The old house is heated entirely by woodburning stoves, which consume several cords of wood through the long New England winters.

Maxine Kumin paused for a few minutes from work to take me around the farm. Our first stop was the paddock behind the barn, where she called her horse over to introduce us. The family has three horses, which they enter regularly in shows and dressage trials. We tramped up to a pasture carved out of the wooded hillside above the house, where the Kumins have made a riding ring for training their horses in the intricate maneuvers of dressage. We saw the vegetable garden, which is enlarged every year as the Kumins cut back more of the encroaching forest; they

grow most of their own food here and in little patches near the house wherever there is sun.

When we returned to the house I noticed gourds drying on the back porch and sunflower seeds tied in cheesecloth bundles hanging from the rafters. Tomato and lettuce plants flourished in a sunny window as we made our way up the narrow stairs to Maxine Kumin's second-floor study. The small, low-ceilinged room has just enough space for a wall of bookshelves, a work surface under the win-

dow, and the writer's large, office-type desk. Framed photographs of horses adorn the walls, along with those of family and friends. I recognized the late poet Anne Sexton as one of them. She once called Kumin "my most dear of friends." A low door opens into the attic room Maxine Kumin has carpeted with a fluffy white rug and furnished minimally with sofa and bookshelf. It is her quiet place, where she retreats from the distractions of farm and family, to read or meditate.

Maxine Kumin (1925–   )—b. Philadelphia, Pennsylvania.
Major works: *Sebastian and the Dragon, The Beach Before Breakfast, Halfway, Up Country: Poems of New England* (1973 Pulitzer Prize), *The Designated Heir* (novel), *The Retrieval System.*

She lives in Warner, New Hampshire.

"Today I trade my last unwise
 ewe lamb, the one who won't leave home,
 for two cords of stove-length oak
 and wait on the old enclosed
 front porch to make the swap.
 November sun revives the thick
 trapped buzz of horseflies. The siren
 for noon and forest fires blows
 a sliding scale. The lamb of woe
 looks in at me through glass
 on the last day of her life."

—*"How It Goes On"*

*The small doorway on the left is the poet's
entrance to her very private space under the eaves.*

*"The night the shift key locked
on my typewriter
and I was at the mercy
of capital letters
a heron marched off the platen
on his unwieldy gear.
The paper birches undressed.
My mare came into the kitchen
and took off her sharp shoes
one by one
and with my index fingernail
I etched I LOVE YOU
on the foolscap of your back."*

—*"The Eight-Hour Dance"*

Maurice Sendak

" *Once Jennie had everything. She slept on a round pillow upstairs and a square pillow downstairs. She had her own comb and brush, two different bottles of pills, eyedrops, eardrops, a thermometer, and for cold weather a red wool sweater. There were two windows for her to look out of and two bowls to eat from. She even had a master who loved her. But Jennie didn't care.* **"**

—Higglety Pigglety Pop!

Maurice Sendak is the same age as his favorite character, Mickey Mouse, and he celebrates that fact by displaying replicas of the Disney mouse all over his studio. Sendak's own characters also have universal appeal. He has never lost touch with the child in himself, and his great gift is his spirited articulation of our deepest childhood fantasies, verbally and visually. Sendak has illustrated more than eighty children's books, including the dozen or so he has written.

Sendak's spacious gray frame house in Connecticut has one wing that was built in 1790. Old trees, dogwoods, and flowering shrubbery screen it from the country road that ambles along one side, and the house is surrounded by an acre or so of lawn and gardens, an ideal playground for Sendak's three dogs, Aggie, Erda, and Io.

When I visited him there, I was surprised to see how orderly his studio was. He has an apartment in New York City but finds that he works best in the rural setting. Sendak's many-windowed studio is approached through the kitchen and down a short flight of steps. Though filled with whimsical toys, drawings, posters, and prints, it is an "all-business" kind of place with a clean drafting board and sharpened pencils. When Sendak is working intensively on a project he hardly leaves this room, listening to Mozart while he draws and preferring silence when he writes.

An avid book collector, Maurice Sendak owns the complete first editions of Herman Melville and Henry James and has shelves full of the Big Little Books of the 1930s, featuring Flash Gordon and Mickey Mouse. Sendak dates his love of books and bookmaking from the moment in early childhood when he received his first fine book, a gift from his sister. He remembers staring at it for a long time and then biting and smelling it. Those early pleasures are still Maurice Sendak's best reason for producing beautiful books for children.

Maurice Sendak (1928–)—b. Brooklyn, New York.
Major works: *The Sign on Rosie's Door, Nutshell Library, Where the Wild Things Are* (1964 Caldecott Medal), *Higglety Pigglety Pop!, Or There Must Be More to Life, In the Night Kitchen.*

He lives in Ridgefield, Connecticut.

Maurice Sendak's workroom is dominated by a colorful Winsor McCay poster of a Gulliver-like figure surrounded by little people, not unlike Sendak himself, who is surrounded by his own and Disney's characters, including stuffed Wild Things and a pillow embroidered with Night Kitchen's Mickey.

Annie Dillard

"You can't picture it, can you? Neither can I. Oh, the desk is yellow, the oak table round, the ferns alive, the mirror cold, and I have never cared. I read. In the Middle Ages, I read, 'the idea of a thing which a man framed for himself was always more real to him than the actual thing itself.' Of course. I am in my Middle Ages; the world at my feet, the world through the window, is an illuminated manuscript whose leaves the wind takes, one by one, whose painted illuminations and halting words draw me, one by one, and I am dazzled in days and lost."

—Holy the Firm

Annie Dillard can make a home anywhere; she now lives on a tree-lined street in a Connecticut college town. She is not the druid and sorceress I had conjured up after reading her books. When she lived on Tinker Creek in Virginia she likened herself to an anchorite and wrote, "Some anchor holds were simple sheds clamped to the side of a church like a barnacle to a rock. I think of this house clamped to the side of Tinker Creek as an anchor hold." Later, having moved to a remote bay near Puget Sound, she wrote, "I came here to study hard things—rock mountain and salt sea—and to temper my spirit on their edges." When I visited her, Annie Dillard was teaching at a university and had recently moved into a college-owned pink stucco house on a quiet street, a stone's throw from the campus.

The writer's study was on the second floor and she was just now beginning to feel comfortable in it, although, she pointed out, it was uncharacteristically tidy. She laughed and said, "But I'm not going to fake it for the picture and make it messy." The most important accessories to her work have followed her through her recent vagabond years in a small trunk. They are her journals and indexed records of everything she has read since she was eighteen. They are extremely important to her for information, "and that's what a writer needs, isn't it?"

Annie Dillard (1945–   )—b. Pittsburg, Pennsylvania.
Major works: *Pilgrim at Tinker Creek* (1974 Pulitzer Prize), *Holy the Firm.*

She lives in Middletown, Connecticut.

When she is writing, the author draws the curtains in her study because she is always tempted by the outdoors. Among the first items to be unpacked in the new house are her journals and notes, all in meticulous order and detail.

One of the treasures from Annie Dillard's trunk is an illuminated draft of a manuscript, attesting to her graphic as well as writing talent.

Washington Irving

"I had hoped before this to see you at my little Dutch cottage on the Hudson. Whenever you are in this quarter, and can steal a little interval from the 'Cares of Empire,' come up then, and I will shew you a little nest in which I enjoy more comfort and quietude of mind than I fear you will experience in the White House. **"**

—From a letter to Martin Van Buren, 1836

Engraving of Washington Irving by John Sartain courtesy New York Public Library.

Washington Irving's Hudson River home, Sunnyside, was often so full of guests that the bachelor writer was forced to sleep in his ground-floor study. When Irving bought the old farmhouse in 1835, this possibility had been considered and the romantically draped alcove, a reminder of Irving's days in Moorish Spain as a government attaché, became an important detail in his remodeling plans. As the hub of the house, the writer's study was placed adjacent to the front door and had a fine view downriver toward New York City, his former home. Here Irving wrote at the desk given to him by his publisher, G. P. Putnam, and he could hear carriage wheels turning in the drive, announcing the arrival of visitors.

Irving wrote to his brother:

"I am living most cozily and delightfully in this bright little home, which I have fitted up to my own humor. Everything goes on cheerily in my little household, and I would not exchange the cottage for any château in Christendom. I am working, too, with almost as much industry and rapidity as I did at Hell Gate, and, I think, will more than pay for my nest, from the greater number of eggs I shall be able to hatch there."

Sunnyside hugs the riverbank and is decidedly Dutch in feeling in spite of being a composite of the architectural fancies of Irving's day. From the wide lawns it is easy to look out on the Tappan Zee, where the river widens into a playground for small sailboats. North of the house one can look toward Sleepy Hollow and recall Katrina Van Tassel, Rip Van Winkle, Ichabod Crane, and the Headless Horseman, Washington Irving's best-loved characters.

Washington Irving (1783–1859)—b. New York City, New York.
Major works: *The Sketch Book of Geoffrey Crayon, Gent.; Tales of a Traveller; The Legend of the Alhambra; A Book of the Hudson; Life of George Washington.*

"Sunnyside," West Sunnyside Lane, Tarrytown, New York, open to the public.

A remarkably old and gnarled wisteria vine,
planted in Irving's time, and three charming weathervanes
greet visitors today at Sunnyside.

Irving used the study at Sunnyside as his sleeping quarters until the addition of a three-story tower provided four more bedrooms for the overflow of guests and servants.

The writer's cape and top hat still hang in the foyer outside his study door.

Edgar Allan Poe

"[The ideal chamber] is oblong . . . curtains of an exceedingly rich crimson silk, fringed with a deep network of gold, and lined with silver tissue. . . . The carpet . . . is quite half an inch thick. Two large sofas of rosewood and crimson silk, gold flowered . . . A pianoforte. Four large and gorgeous Sèvres vases, in which bloom a profusion of sweet and vivid flowers . . . an Argand lamp, with a plain crimson-tinted ground-glass shade . . . throws a tranquil but magical radiance over all."

—The Philosophy of Furniture

(*Courtesy Bronx County Historical Society.*)

Chills ran up his arm when French surrealist painter René Magritte touched Edgar Allan Poe's rocking chair on a visit to the writer's four-room farmhouse in the Bronx. But then, the French have always been more sensitive than most to Poe's macabre genius.

The restless author, orphaned at an early age, was born in Massachusetts but grew up in Richmond, Virginia, and worked as an editor there as well as in Baltimore and Philadelphia. When "The Raven" was published in 1845, Poe was acclaimed internationally and became owner and editor of a literary weekly in New York City, where he had been working on the *Mirror*. His *Broadway Journal* collapsed after one year, but during that time Poe had moved to the house in the Fordham area of the Bronx because it was on high ground and he hoped it would provide a healthier climate away from the crowded city for his young wife, Virginia, who was dying of tuberculosis.

Edgar Allan Poe wrote very little during his three years at the Bronx cottage, but "Annabel Lee," "The Bells," and "Ulalume" were composed there in the small attic room the poet reached by climbing the narrow flight of stairs outside Virginia's bedroom door.

I visited the Poe cottage on a winter day and was conscious of a damp chill that penetrated the uninsulated walls of the meager structure. It reminded me of the description of the terrible last days of the poet's wife, whose only warmth on her deathbed was from her husband's cloak and from the family cat nestled on her breast.

Edgar Allan Poe (1809–1849)—b. Boston, Massachusetts.
Major works: *Tamerlane and Other Poems, Tales of the Grotesque and Arabesque,* "Ulalume," "The Philosophy of Composition," *Eureka.*

The Edgar Allan Poe Cottage, Grand Concourse at East 193rd Street, Bronx, New York, open to the public. The Poe Museum, 1914 East Main Street, Richmond, Virginia, containing reminders of Poe's childhood in this city and his job with the *Southern Literary Messenger,* open to the public.
The Edgar Allan Poe House, 203 Amity Street, Baltimore, Maryland, and the Edgar Allan Poe House, 530 North Seventh Street, Philadelphia, Pennsylvania, open to the public.

Poe wrote "Annabel Lee" at his cottage in the Bronx and dedicated it to his wife, Virginia. She died within the year, and the despondent Poe died two years later in Richmond, Virginia.

The bed and the parlor rocker are the only pieces of furniture that belonged to the Poes when they occupied the Fordham cottage; many of their household possessions were sold off to pay for food.

Zane Grey

" A mile or so from its mouth the Lackawaxen leaves the shelter of the hills and seeks the open sunlight and slows down to widen into long lanes that glide reluctantly over the few last restraining barriers to the Delaware. In a curve between two of these level lanes, there is a place where barefoot boys wade and fish for chubs and bask on the big boulders like turtles. "

—The Lord of Lackawaxen Creek

Would Americans have made him the best-selling novelist of all time if his name had remained Pearl Grey? Not likely. As a young man Zane Grey made two remarkable decisions that changed the direction of his life. First he dropped his given name in favor of the more rugged-sounding ancestral name "Zane," and then, with his wife Lina's encouragement, he abandoned a successful dental practice in New York City for a writing career in the wilds of Pennsylvania.

But the writing didn't flow until Grey met Buffalo Jones, one of the last of the plainsmen, who took him on an extensive trip through the far West, where Grey became "possessed," in his words, by its magnificence. Back in his home in Lackawaxen, Pennsylvania, Zane Grey sat day and night in his Morris chair with a lapboard across the arms, and wrote by hand on lined yellow paper his first western novel, *Last of the Plainsmen*. This was followed by *The Heritage of the Desert* and *Riders of the Purple Sage*, which sold over two million

Photo of Zane Grey courtesy Zane Grey Museum.

copies in the first few years after its publication in 1912. As his fame grew, Grey spent most of his time in the West, and during his lifetime wrote an astonishing total of eighty-six books. His love of the outdoors was

also manifested in a vast number of articles published with such compelling titles as "Roping Lions in the Grand Canyon," "Fighting Swordfish," and "Bear Chasing," all drawn from the writer's own experience.

Zane Grey's rambling frame house in Lackawaxen was inherited by Mrs. Helen Johnson, the daughter of Alvah James, Grey's friend who arranged that significant meeting with Buffalo Jones. Here, in this beautiful and remote area of the Delaware River Valley, frequently visited by fishermen and small-game hunters, she has created a small museum honoring one of the great sportsmen of all time.

Zane Grey (1872–1939)—b. Zanesville, Ohio.
Major works: *The Spirit of the Border, The Last of the Plainsmen, The Heritage of the Desert, Riders of the Purple Sage, Tales of Fishing.*

Zane Grey Museum, Lackawaxen, Pennsylvania, open to the public.

Memorabilia in Grey's former home include many of his souvenirs from the West and copies of his most popular novels.

H. L. Mencken

> **"***It is impossible to state categorically what produces the stimulus to write. I assume that it is inborn. Some people have it and others do not. Ideas for books and articles come to me. . . . I always have in hand at least one-hundred times as many as I could conceivably execute.***"**
>
> —From a letter to B. Othanel Smith, Esq., 1938

A portrait of Mencken at forty-seven by Nikol Schattenstein hangs among specially bound editions of his numerous works and his one hundred and six buckram scrapbooks, meticulously filled by the author.

The irreverent "Sage of Baltimore" was a fine bricklayer, I discovered while poking around the backyard of H. L. Mencken's row house in Baltimore. Gardening was another tranquil hobby of the fiery Mencken, editor, journalist, critic, satirist, encyclopedist, and spokesman for an era.

Mencken's house was left to the University of Maryland by the writer's brother, August, when he died, and the large, graceful, high-ceilinged rooms are now almost empty. Mencken's third-floor study, famous for its clutter and the scene of his amazing productivity, is now occupied by a graduate student.

The garden behind the house is where I had a strong sense of the writer's remarkable energy. Here, he and August spent long hours building paths and walls of brick, inlaid with pieces of tile, mathematical formulas, and a death mask of Beethoven along with the opening bars of the Fifth Symphony, a tribute to H. L. Mencken's love of music. Mencken enjoyed working in the garden, weeding the flower beds, chopping wood, and stacking it neatly near the kitchen door. This was a place he habitually went to to relax and meditate.

No institutions and few leading figures of his time were immune to the insults and biting wit of the legendary Mencken, and it surprised me to learn that his own domestic life had been so circumscribed. H. L. Mencken lived at 1524 Hollins Street for all but eight years of his life.

Henry Louis Mencken
(1880–1956)—b. Baltimore, Maryland.
Major works: *The American Language, Happy Days, Newspaper Days, Heathen Days.*

The Mencken House, 1524 Hollins Street, Baltimore, Maryland, owned by the University of Maryland, by appointment only.
The Mencken Room of the Enoch Pratt Free Library, Baltimore, Maryland, houses Mencken's huge collection of scrapbooks, his library, and other memorabilia.

Handsome arched doorway in foreground is 1524 Hollins Street, Mencken's typical Baltimore rowhouse.

The Sage's small 1910 Corona (below) on which he wrote most of his books is now housed in the Mencken room of Baltimore's Enoch Pratt Free Library.

Mencken's garden wall was studded with mathematical formulae, family coats-of-arms, Beethoven's mask, and the opening bars of the Fifth Symphony.

William Carlos Williams

"_Dr. Wood, our dentist and a fellow Penn alumnus, told me one day casually, as though in passing, that he wanted me to buy his house at Nine Ridge Road. In my wildest imagination I hadn't even thought of such a thing. . . . I objected that I couldn't afford such a house, one of the most prominent in town. . . . Neither Floss nor I shall ever forget the day we moved in. You might think it had been the palace of one of the Medici._**"**

—The Autobiography of William Carlos Williams

A family photograph of William Carlos Williams hangs in the house.

There are poignant reminders of William Carlos Williams at 9 Ridge Road in Rutherford, New Jersey. The poet died in 1963, and although his books and possessions have been carted away to libraries and his son now lives in the sprawling, mustard-color clapboard house, relics of Williams' involvement in the arts of the early twentieth century remain.

Dr. William Eric Williams—Bill—showed me the attic work space used by his father for writing in the 1920s. Gallery notices, cartoons, photos, posters, and children's drawings are still randomly tacked to the stained beaverboard walls. His father built the stand-up desk top against one wall to provide for a refreshing change of posture while writing; a coal stove for heat in winter, a heavy desk, typewriter, and backless stool, with a single lamp dangling from the ceiling, complete the picture of the room in those earlier days. Bill Williams still remembers the poet's hunt-and-jab system of typing, which sounded as if he were "beating the hell out of the machine."

The garden behind the house is still cultivated much as it must have been when William Carlos Williams would escape from his desk to spend an hour or two turning the soil or laying the uneven stone walk which brings people from the garage to the back door of the house, the family's main entrance. Bill Williams continues to practice medicine in the office, just inside the back door and to the right, that his father used for so many years.

Williams was an unusual man. He was not only a Pulitzer Prize–winning poet, but an important essayist, novelist, and playwright who published almost fifty books during his lifetime and founded the avant-garde magazine _Contact_. He practiced pediatric medicine in Rutherford, and yet he knew most of the important artists of his day, including Ezra Pound, Gertrude Stein, Alfred Stieglitz, Marianne Moore, Charles Demuth, Marsden Hartley, and Berenice Abbott, all of whom, like Williams, were participants in the creation of a distinctly American expression in the arts.

William Carlos Williams
(1883–1963)—b. Rutherford, New Jersey.
Major works: Poetry: _Kora in Hell: Improvisations, Paterson I–V, Pictures from Brueghel_ (1963 Pulitzer Prize). Fiction: _A Voyage to Pagany, Life Along the Passaic River_. Nonfiction: _In the American Grain, Selected Essays, The Autobiography of William Carlos Williams_.

The Williams house at 9 Ridge Road, Rutherford, New Jersey, on the National Register of Historic Places, not open to the public.

Nine Ridge Road has always been painted a light mustard color. The front entrance was almost never used by the Williams family, who preferred the back door on the house's garden side.

The six-by-twelve-foot mural of Manhattan's East Side by Eyvind Earle is a fitting reminder of Williams' involvement in the New York art world during the first half of the twentieth century.

The poet's familiar Panama hat rests on the heavy wooden desk where he wrote much of his work after long office hours. The desk is now in the Rutherford Public Library.

"As a writer I have never felt that medicine interfered with me but rather that it was my very food and drink, the very thing which made it possible for me to write. Was I not interested in man? . . . I knew it wasn't for the most part giving me anything very profound, but it was giving me terms, basic terms with which I could spell out matters as profound as I cared to think of."

—The Autobiography of William Carlos Williams

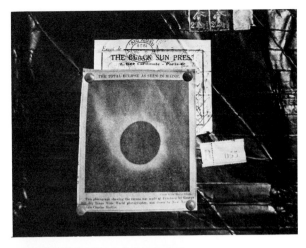

The north and south walls of the poet's attic studio are covered with posters, photographs, gallery announcements, and cartoons, including a four-foot graph of New York Stock Exchange activity from 1928 to 1932. The six-foot-long, chest-high desk was built by Williams himself.

Marianne Moore

> **"** *I do not write for money or fame. . . . One writes because one has a burning desire to objectify what is indispensable to one's happiness to express.* **"**
>
> —"Idiosyncrasy and Technique"

Photo of Marianne Moore courtesy Rosenbach Museum and Library, Marianne Moore Collection.

Marianne Moore's apartment has moved. Like her beloved Brooklyn Dodgers, her things have been packed up and moved to another town. In Philadelphia, at the Rosenbach Foundation, the living room of her Greenwich Village apartment, where she lived for the last seven years of her life, has been meticulously re-created in every detail.

Marianne Moore's name was synonymous with Brooklyn for the thirty-five years she lived there at 260 Cumberland Street. This was after the *Dial*, the outstanding avant-garde literary review of the day, closed its doors for the final time in 1929, leaving Miss Moore, its editor, free to spend her mornings writing and to work part-time in the New York Public Library.

"I have a mania for straight writing—however circuitous I may be in what I myself say of plants, animals, or places. . . . I mean, in part, writing that is not mannered, over-conscious, or at war with common sense." "Straight" was what I expected Marianne Moore's apartment to be, and in a sense it is, with the rather formal Empire and Chippendale furniture, the handsome mantel clock and fine drawings. But there are a lot of whimsical surprises that make the room an extremely personal expression. Small animals and odd creatures are everywhere, revealing Moore's partiality for reptiles, especially dragons. Her desk from the *Dial* sits under one of the long windows near the folding Morris chair she often used with a lapboard when writing at home. Miss Moore kept fit with a daily workout on the trapeze in the doorway, and her large collection of phonograph records includes jazz as well as classical music. There is a blue velvet footstool given to the poet by T. S. Eliot and, of course, the inevitable—autographed baseballs.

Marianne Moore (1887–1972) —b. St. Louis, Missouri. **Major works:** *Poems, The Pangolin and Other Verse, What Are Years, Collected Poems* (1951 Bollingen Prize and Pulitzer Prize), *The Fables of La Fontaine* (translation), *Complete Poems.*

The Phillip H. & A. S. W. Rosenbach Foundation, 2010 De Lancey Place, Philadelphia, Pennsylvania, is the home of Marianne Moore's personal possessions and manuscripts. Her room is open to the public by appointment.

Miss Moore's famous
tricorn hat sits atop
her "Bryn Mawr
desk," the one she
used during her
college years. Above
it are drawings by
William Blake and an
oil painting from her
grandfather's home in
Missouri.

Amid the vast collection of small animals is an autographed baseball, a gift from Joe DiMaggio and Mickey Mantle on the poet's birthday.

Marianne Moore's desk from her Dial *days (1925–1929) seems
dwarfed by the newfangled electric typewriter.*

Edna St. Vincent Millay

" *We decided after all to postpone the installation of our individual bath until the dormer windows are in and the installation of the dormer windows until the terrace is laid and the laying of the terrace until the swimming pool is dug and the digging of the swimming pool until we get enough money to buy some cocoa-butter against sunburn.* **"**

—From a letter, 1925

Photo of Edna St. Vincent Millay courtesy Millay Colony for the Arts.

The romantic beauty of Steepletop is haunting. Edna St. Vincent Millay's estate high on a mountain in the Berkshires, which she and her husband built and farmed for more than thirty years, is now the Millay Colony for the Arts, a subsidized working retreat for artists and writers.

Millay, one of the best-loved writers of the 1920s, whose verse celebrated love and freedom with a lyric freshness, immersed herself in horticulture and the seasonal activities of the farm, which she duly noted in her poems. The couple entertained frequently, and over the years outbuildings, a gazebo, a pool, and a barn were added as well as a one-room cabin in the woods, where the poet would retire to write. "I have a shanty up in the field where I work," she wrote to Edmund Wilson. "I'm in my shanty now, and have a scorching fire at my back, in the funniest little stove."

Norma Millay Ellis, the poet's sister, now lives at Steepletop, and after allowing me to wander and photograph at a leisurely pace one June day, she led me up the steep path behind the main house to see roses and lilies and clumps of strawberries planted by Edna St. Vincent Millay more than thirty years ago and still thriving in the climate of Steepletop.

Edna St. Vincent Millay (1892–1950)—b. Rockland, Maine. **Major works:** *Renascence and Other Poems, The Harp Weaver and Other Poems* (1923 Pulitzer Prize), *Conversation at Midnight, Collected Poems.*

Millay Colony for the Arts, Steepletop, Austerlitz, New York, by appointment only.

A statue
of Diana
stands guard
at Steepletop,
a fitting
reminder of
the writer
who was
often called
the poet
of love.

"Time after time I got up out of bed in the middle of the night, and sighed, and picked up a couple of blankets and a pillow, and trudged up to my cabin in the pines, and tried to sleep there. But there is no bed there, not even a couch, just a rather small chaise-longue. So I haven't had much sleep this winter."

—From a letter, 1950

Gordon Parks

"I sit now drowning in the music of Ravel, looking out on the slow-moving river. Jagged patches of ice—like parts of a huge broken white bird—float downstream to the sea. On the shore, a lone woman clad entirely in black dances crazily, stopping now and then to kick up snow in her fury. . . . I watch, fascinated—yet a little fearful—as she moves closer to the waterside. The river flows, the woman dances—both to the rhythm of Ravel, which neither can hear."

—To Smile in Autumn

"I feel rather silly coming to take *your* picture," I mumbled to writer-photographer Gordon Parks as he greeted me at the door of his sunny apartment in one of Manhattan's elegant steel-and-glass towers.

Parks could easily be called a present-day Renaissance man. From a bleak childhood in Kansas he overcame discrimination and poverty to become one of this country's best-known photographers. Adding to his career as a celebrated photojournalist for *Life* magazine, Parks wrote several books of poems and a piano concerto. The success of his book *The Learning Tree* opened a career in film-making for Gordon Parks; he produced and directed an adaptation of it and subsequently four other films. "I have never refused a new assignment or a new challenge," he says.

Gordon Parks's home is a very personal aerie crowded with the memorabilia and appurtenances of an active life: medals and awards, photographs of family and friends, sculpture and paintings by people he knows, a grand piano alongside large color blowups of his favorite photographs. Honorary degrees hang beside a pair of ski boots; a camera rests on his desk next to a freshly typed manuscript.

Parks was revising the manuscript of his latest book in his study when I arrived. Classical music from the stereo set enveloped the room. Music is an important part of the creative process for Parks, who has always played the piano. He uses it to set the mood, and as he works late into the night at his typewriter he listens to favorite concertos with earphones. Pointing to the floor-to-ceiling wall of glass overlooking the East River, Parks described his writing habits. "Usually in the mornings the sun is there and I get up, come in here, and review what I wrote the day before." He sprawled in a huge, sheepskin-covered armchair by the window and began to correct his work. "Usually all of my mistakes come to me in this chair. It is my truth chair."

Gordon Parks (1912–   )—b. Fort Scott, Kansas.
Major works: *The Learning Tree, A Choice of Weapons, A Poet and His Camera, Whispers of Intimate Things, Born Black, Moments Without Proper Names, Flavio, To Smile in Autumn.*

He lives in New York City.

John Jay Osborn, Jr.

"_What a nice place," Camilla Newman was able to say, even though she had a finger in her mouth. "I like all this Indian stuff, all the hangings and the blankets. And it doesn't look legal."_

"I'm so glad you approve," Littlefield said. "This bohemian palace reveals my split personality.**"**

—The Associates

What is the writer who immortalized Harvard Law School doing with a Yale banner over his desk?

John Jay Osborn, Jr.'s allegiance is divided. He has degrees from both schools. Osborn, who was named for the first Supreme Court Justice, John Jay, awakened popular interest in the legal profession with a movie and two recent television series taken from his novels *The Paper Chase* and *The Associates.*

John Osborn and his family live in a small frame Victorian house, painted a deep ocher, which was once the gatekeeper's cottage of a Hudson River estate. His workroom is upstairs, tucked under the high, dormered roof. The corner room has two windows that face the road but he is not easily distracted by the sounds of his young son, Sam, at play, or the family's husky dog, Josh, sleeping under his desk. "This is a completely self-contained environment," he said as he showed me his color television set, a stereo tape deck, his reference library of law books. "The only thing I have to go out to get is a beer."

Osborn writes, "when I'm hot," for seven or eight hours a day, starting in the early morning. In winter, when the wind blows off the Hudson and whistles through the thin cottage walls, he wears his favorite down vest as a good-luck talisman and only incidentally to keep warm.

John Jay Osborn, Jr. (1945–   )—b. Boston, Massachusetts.
Major works: *The Paper Chase, The Only Thing I've Done Wrong, The Associates.*

He lives in the Riverdale section of the Bronx, New York.

Carl Sandburg

"Here among his own trees, bushes, paths, with no interfering street lights, he could be alone with the moon, with the latticed crossplay of shadows, with the timeless patterns of black patch and silver curve flowing to the confluence of branches, leaves, and moonfall to the earth, each pattern silent, current, yet infinitely transient."

—Remembrance Rock

"Don't ever lose the country in you," advised a retired city slicker I met in the barnyard at Connemara, the alpine farm in North Carolina where, after more than fifty years in the Midwest, Carl Sandburg spent the last quarter of his life. My fellow tourist had a point.

Certainly Carl Sandburg, poet, historian, novelist, songwriter, and minstrel, never lost the country in him.

"I was born on the prairie and the milk of its wheat, the red of its clover, the eyes of its women, gave me a song and a slogan," he wrote in *Cornhuskers*. It seems ironical that Sandburg's Chicago poems commemorating the ills and vitality of the industrial society were what made him famous.

Connemara, the secluded farm on Big and Little Glassy mountains, appealed to the Sandburg family for its gentle climate and its ample pasture land, ideal for the prize-winning Chikaming goats that Mrs. Sandburg grew here. She and her daughters ran the farm while Carl Sandburg pursued his writing career undisturbed.

A visitor to Connemara cannot help being impressed by its simplicity. The pre–Civil War house of more than thirty rooms is furnished sparely with comfortable stuffed furniture of indeterminate age, utilitarian desks and worktables in every room, bookshelves to the ceiling wherever possible to hold the family's twelve thousand books, a phonograph, and

Portrait of Carl Sandburg by Jan Clausing.

record albums stacked in just about every room. There are no curtains at the large windows because the family preferred to see the trees and sky. Photographs and favorite pictures clipped from magazines, tacked in groups on masonite board, are the rooms' only embellishment. Even with no one living there the house radiates warmth and a feeling of a busy, happy family life.

Carl Sandburg's life at Connemara was a mix of work and simple family pleasures, such as reading aloud or singing together after dinner. Late in the evenings, the poet would climb the stairs to his cluttered workroom on the third floor. There, wearing a green eyeshade and chewing on a cigar, Sandburg would often work at his typewriter until dawn,

sometimes waving from his attic window to the family as they went off to the goat barns to do the morning milking.

During these years Sandburg also spent a lot of time traveling around the country lecturing and making public appearances, and it was always his delight to return to the peace of Connemara, where, Harry Golden said of his friend and neighbor, "There are days he stuffs wrapped sandwiches in his pocket and disappears into the woods to experience silence and loneliness—and wonder."

Carl Sandburg (1878–1967)—b. Galesburg, Illinois.
Major works: *Cornhuskers, Abraham Lincoln, The American Songbag, Rootabaga Stories, Abraham Lincoln: The War Years* (1939 Pulitzer Prize), *Complete Poems* (1950 Pulitzer Prize).

The Carl Sandburg Birthplace, 331 East Third Street, Galesburg, Illinois, open to the public.
The Carl Sandburg Home National Historic Site, Flat Rock, North Carolina, open to the public.

you might have more
with your soul and
...t you like, thus adding
...ich is somewhat re-
...e-ness of school-study,
...d the work and will not
...uncongenial study of
..., and if you feel that
...the teaching field and
...to a life-work, why

...trictly a woman's
...s her presence hon-
...r. But we're put
...as we can be so
...the happiness of
...w should probably
...h situation is at
...emperament.

build up your personality. Of such," it seems
to me mrs. Whipple is one of the most potent
influences that you have met. However, you
don't know what you may yet meet in Albany.

However, it really doesn't matter much
which way you decide. Happiness has its source
in the soul, in individuality, and if you're my true
sister, you will live much of an out-door-life,
scatter your love, your smiles and your quiet
jests hither and hence willy-nilly, not car-
ing a jot or tittle whether they light on stony
ground or not.
How oft like Cyrano, I faced a hundred men, to fight
alone and single-handed them a pallid, starlit night;
But unlike Cyrano, when morning stars broke out in song,
Baffled, baggageless and sore, I found that I was lost in flight.

Here is love to you, sister. And whatever your
own deepest instinct tell... ..., that is right.

Charlie.

Carl Sandburg's study reflects the
simplicity of the man. Manuscripts and
letters from his huge correspondence are
carefully organized and filed in painted
orange crates. His typewriter rests on an
unpainted crate and the wood stove still
contains hundreds of the writer's cigar
butts.

Sandburg's taste in wall decoration was as simple as his taste in furniture. His granddaughter Paula Steichen recalls one wall of his bedroom "entirely covered with pictures clipped from magazines—some three layers deep."

Family heirlooms are explained in this handwritten note from Sandburg to his daughters.

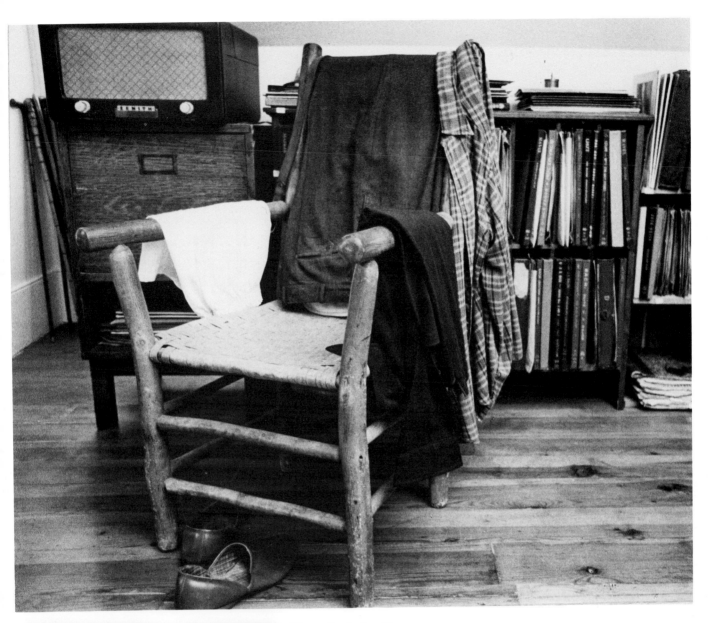

The writer's familiar
checked shirt and
carpet slippers in
a corner of his
bedroom, where he
would listen to
phonograph records
from his extensive
library of classical
music.

William Faulkner

" . . . this land, this South, for which God has done so much, with woods for game and streams for fish and deep rich soil for seed and lush springs to sprout it and long summers to mature it and serene falls to harvest it and short mild winters for men and animals. "

—The Hamlet

Oxford, Mississippi, is the Lafayette County seat and the hometown of two Faulkner brothers who were writers. I suspect that until recently people around Oxford knew more about brother John's less distinguished but more easily appreciated work because brother Billy was a somewhat aloof character.

William Faulkner seemed to prefer it that way. His obsession for privacy gave the town very little to talk about. "It is my ambition to be, as a private individual, abolished and voided from history, leaving it markless, no refuse save the printed books," he wrote to editor and writer Malcolm Cowley. Yet few other writers have mined the resources of their home region more than William Faulkner. He made his part of the South immortal.

Faulkner's great-grandfather, the legendary old Colonel Falkner, was the founder of the family fortune in Mississippi. He fought heroically in the Civil War, built railroads, farmed, and wrote novels, but his death by an assassin's bullet in 1889 began the decline of the family's social influence.

Sartoris, William Faulkner's third novel and his first about the people of the imaginary Yoknapatawpha County, convinced him that he could build a life's work around the story of a genteel Southern family faced with the rise of industrial society, a theme that was to run through most of his work.

Painting of William Faulkner by Murray Lloyd Goldsborough, 1962, courtesy University of Mississippi Library.

With a copy of Faulkner's own hand-drawn map of Yoknapatawpha County in hand, I roamed the country around Oxford, trying to find some of the scenes familiar in his work. Oxford is a busy university town, with a thriving community of attractive shops and restaurants around the old courthouse square. There on the courthouse steps or on the benches beneath the trees, William Faulkner as a boy heard the local folk swapping the tall tales and legends that he later wove into his work.

Rowan Oak, the writer's home about a mile outside of Oxford, was a dilapidated antebellum house when the Faulkners bought it in 1930, and it proved a never-ending drain on his then scant financial resources. Faulkner did most of the restoration work himself, and though it looks almost grand in pictures, in reality it is a modest two-storied, four-bedroom house.

The writer built his study at the back, on the ground floor. It has a daybed, some books, two small desks, one of which was made for him by his stepson, and a fireplace with an electric grate. The most interesting feature of the room is the outline for his novel *A Fable*, which Faulkner wrote in his own hand on the wall above the daybed. "I usually get to work pretty early in the morning, and by 10:30 or 11 I'm through," Faulkner once told an interviewer. "But I can sit down and write almost any time. The stories seem to shape themselves."

From the two windows of his study he could see the paddock and stable. "I am not really a writer," William Faulkner once said. "I'm a countryman. My life is farmland and horses and the raising of feed and grain. I took up writing simply because I liked it."

The denizens of Oxford now admit that the arrival of the MGM movie crew in 1949 to film *Intruder in the Dust* was what caused them to take notice of brother Billy's growing acclaim. He was awarded the 1949 Nobel Prize.

Rowan Oak, the nineteenth-century plantation restored by Faulkner in the 1930s as a horse farm and family home, was his refuge from the world until the end of his life.

William Faulkner (1897–1962)—b. New Albany, Mississippi.
Major works: *Sartoris, The Sound and the Fury, As I Lay Dying, Sanctuary, Light in August, Absalom, Absalom!, The Hamlet.*

Rowan Oak, owned by the University of Mississippi, open to the public when the university is in session.

Portrait of the author hangs in the living room of the family home in Oxford.

WEDNESDAY

I — The Regiment is brought to Chaulnesmont, under arrest, and put into the prison compound. Magdalen is in the crowd waiting for the quarrel. Introduces the Corporal and his squad and the three Generals.

IV — The German General is flown across the lines at Villeneuve l'Abbaye, shot at with blank archie and pursued by the three British aeroplanes firing blank ammunition. Levine's story included.

V — The Division Commander is brought to Chaulnesmont, under arrest.

VII — Many and Martha reach Chaulnesmont and are met by Magdalen. They are repulsed by the people in the city because of their relationship to the Corporal, whom the people hold responsible for the Regiment's mutiny and hence the present jeopardy.

VI — 17:00 The Runner finds himself free of arrest, escapes to the rear, and sees the German aeroplane, surrounded by false anti-aircraft fire and pursued by the three British aeroplanes firing blank ammunition, land on the aerodrome at Villeneuve l'Abbaye. Includes the story of the Runner, the Sentry, the old Negro preacher and his grandson and the Shiloh Race horse.

VII — The Prisoners in the Compound.

VII — The Division Commander is put under arrest by the Old General.

VII — The Old General and witnesses examine the Corporal.

VII — The Old General's interview with Mary, Martha and Magdalen. Martha's story.

VII — The 3 Generals and the German General.

VII — The story of the Old General and his Quarter Master General.

VII — The Old General seals her aide to repeat the miracle of the Spoon.

Faulkner's typewriter sits in a corner of his study with a door beyond providing easy access to the paddock. Over the daybed he wrote an outline of his 1954 novel, A Fable, and used it as a guide.

"Frenchman's Bend was a section of rich river-bottom country lying twenty miles southeast of Jefferson. Hill-cradled and remote, definite yet without boundaries, straddling into two counties and owning allegiance to neither, it had been the original grant and site of a tremendous pre–Civil War plantation, the ruins of which . . . were still known as the Old Frenchman's place."

—The Hamlet

"The courthouse: the center, the focus, the hub; sitting looming in the center of the country's circumference like a single cloud in its ring of horizon."

Thomas Wolfe

> ❝ *I am, he thought, a part of all that I have touched and that has touched me, which, having for me no existence save that which I gave to it, became other than itself by being mixed with what I then was, and is now still otherwise, having fused with what I now am, which is itself a cumulation of what I have been becoming. Why here? Why there? Why now? Why then?* ❞

—Look Homeward, Angel

Photo of Thomas Wolfe and his mother on the porch of Dixieland courtesy Pack Memorial Public Library, Asheville, North Carolina.

*I*f ever there was a writer who didn't need a biographer, that writer is Thomas Wolfe," said his editor, Maxwell Perkins. The gigantic young man from Asheville, North Carolina, wrote a mountain of prose, which when edited by Perkins became Wolfe's first novel, *Look Homeward, Angel.* Published in 1929, the book could be considered autobiography or pure fiction. Wolfe himself wrote in his note to the reader, "If the writer has used the clay of life to make his book, he has only used what all men must, what none can keep from using."

Wolfe's clay was Asheville, now a prosperous Southern city, where a modern high-rise office-and-hotel complex has risen across the street from his mother's boardinghouse. Wolfe described the mountain town when he was a boy as having been "for him the center of the earth, the small but dynamic core of all life."

When I visited Dixieland, the boardinghouse owned and operated by Thomas Wolfe's mother when he was growing up, I felt transported back in time to the simpler days before World War I described in Wolfe's novel. It was for me too, on the morning I visited, a "great chill, tomb," as I entered the "big cheaply constructed frame house of eighteen or twenty drafty high-ceilinged rooms," with a "rambling, unplanned, gabular appearance." But for me there was also the magical feeling of reminiscence, of the pleasure I had when I first read Wolfe's book.

"But we are the sum of all the moments of our lives," Thomas Wolfe wrote in his note to the reader. When he died several years later of tuberculosis, he left behind an eight-foot-high stack of unpublished manuscripts. Wolfe's friend and editor wrote later, "I think no one could understand Thomas Wolfe who had not seen or properly imagined the place in which he was born and grew up."

Thomas Wolfe (1900–1938)—b. Asheville, North Carolina.
Major works: *Look Homeward, Angel; Of Time and the River; The Web and the Rock; You Can't Go Home Again.*

The Thomas Wolfe Memorial, 48 Spruce Street, Asheville, North Carolina, open to the public.

"The construction was after her own plans, and of the cheapest material: it never lost the smell of raw wood, cheap varnish, and flimsy rough plastering."

"The 'cheap boarders,' the animation of feeding, the clatter of plates, the braided clamor of their talk."

—Look Homeward, Angel

"Eliza slept soundly in a small dark room with a window opening on the uncertain light of the back porch ... stacks of old newspapers and magazines were piled in the corners."

"He went out into the hall where a dim light burned and the high walls gave back their grave-damp chill. This, he thought, is the house."

"He did not turn on the light, because he disliked seeing the raw blistered varnish of the dresser and the bent white iron of the bed. It sagged, and the light was dim—he hated dim lights, and the large moths, flapping blindly around on their dusty wings."

—Look Homeward, Angel

Walker Percy

>**"**Come into my cell. Make yourself at home. Take the chair; I'll sit on the cot. No? You prefer to stand by the window? I understand. You like my little view. Have you noticed that the narrower the view the more you can see?**"**

—Lancelot

Walter Percy at his home a few miles from his studio, sitting beneath a portrait by an artist friend, Lyn Hill.

Unlike the alienated characters in his novels, Walker Percy seems to have figured things out pretty well—at least when it comes to places to do his writing. He does not write in an antebellum pigeonnier, as Lancelot Lamar did in Percy's widely acclaimed novel *Lancelot.* He writes in a kitchen. This kitchen belongs to a studio Percy rents near his home in a small Louisiana town about twenty-five miles from New Orleans.

The Percys' home is a graceful, Georgian-style brick house whose wide screened porch overlooks a quiet, muddy bayou and trees hung with Spanish moss. The writer's study there is comfortably furnished with a daybed, his files, a large desk, and armchairs drawn up before a fireplace. This room is for reading and the business side of things. For writing, Walker Percy becomes more solitary and drives to his studio a few miles away.

Percy works regularly at the studio, usually in the mornings. It is furnished casually with an old couch, wicker chairs, and bright posters. The writer (a trained physician who does not practice), whose prose is extremely spare and precise, delights in the unkempt look of the room he has chosen to work in.

Here Walker Percy finds the ideal climate for reflecting and writing. "What's nice about this kitchen is that it's got a cassette player and an icebox. Nobody comes here, nobody cleans up, and nobody bothers me. The dishes haven't been washed since 1977. I don't have any soap."

Walker Percy (1916–   )—b. Birmingham, Alabama.
Major works: *The Moviegoer* (1962 National Book Award), *The Last Gentleman, Love in the Ruins, Lancelot, The Second Coming.*

He lives in Covington, Louisiana.

The novelist writes in the second-floor studio he rents in this building.

Flannery O'Connor

" *When we talk about the writer's country we are liable to forget that no matter what particular country it is, it is inside as well as outside him. . . . To know oneself is to know one's region. It is also to know the world, and it is also, paradoxically, a form of exile from that world.* **"**

—*"The Fiction Writer & His Country" in* Mystery and Manners

At Andalusia, the late Flannery O'Connor's home in rural Georgia, the writer's spirit is very much alive. When I arrived at a motel outside Milledgeville, I telephoned Mrs. Regina O'Connor, Flannery's mother.

"Where is Andalusia?" I asked.

"Where are you?" responded the gentle voice.

"At the motel."

"Why, just look out the door!"

Across the highway and up a winding graveled road I found a plain white farmhouse with a cluster of outbuildings where several peacocks squawked at my arrival. They are descendants of the splendid birds Flannery brought from Florida almost thirty years ago. A pair of noisy geese strutted by to see what the peacocks were complaining so emphatically about, and then ducks and peahens appeared on the scene.

"I have bought me some peafowl and sit on the back steps a good deal studying them," Flannery O'Connor wrote to Elizabeth and Robert Lowell. "I am going to be the World Authority on Peafowl, and I hope to be offered a chair someday at Chicken College."

O'Connor was confined at Andalusia in 1952 by the degenerative disease called lupus, which claimed her life twelve years later, and she and her mother established a strict regime to conserve Flannery's energy for writing. Mrs. O'Connor looked

after the farm while her daughter unfailingly devoted three hours every morning to writing. In her book-lined bedroom on the ground floor of the farmhouse, her desk turned away from the inviting front windows, she wrote about the country people of the Georgia Bible Belt, their strengths and peculiarities. Afternoons at Andalusia were saved for visits with friends and feeding her growing family of birds. Sometimes Flannery O'Connor would set up her easel and paint familiar scenes and still lifes in strong colors laid on the canvas with the bold strokes of a palette knife, "because I don't like to wash the brushes."

Religion was a powerful force in O'Connor's life and work, and this fact hit home for me the next morning just before I left Andalusia. It was early, and the April air was fresh and moist. Ernest, the donkey that Flannery gave her mother one Mother's Day, came to the edge of the pasture to nuzzle my hand. I walked around the barnyard again, looking for one last photograph. There was the motley group of farm buildings—the dairy barn, the typical run-down tenant farmer's bungalow, the hay barn. A peacock cried out from his roost in the loft. Returning to my car, I glanced back toward the barnyard and noticed, for the first time, a large, white plastic cross on the porch of the unoccupied tenant farmer's house. I had my photograph.

Flannery O'Connor (1925–1964) —b. Savannah, Georgia.

Major works: *Wise Blood, A Good Man Is Hard to Find, The Violent Bear It Away, Everything That Rises Must Converge, Mystery and Manners: Occasional Prose, The Complete Stories* (1971 National Book Award).

The Ina Dillard Russell Library at Georgia College, Milledgeville, Georgia, contains the Flannery O'Connor Collection of the author's books, manuscripts, critical writings, photographs, and other memorabilia as well as her personal library and some family furniture. The Flannery O'Connor Memorial Room at the library is open to the public. Andalusia, her home near Milledgeville, Georgia, is not open to the public.

"We are expecting the photographer from Holiday to come tomorrow to take the peafowls' pictures. I am sure that the scoundrels will sulk or spread only in front of the garbage can or all go off in the woods until he leaves, and as my mother points out, there is nowhere on this place that you can get a picture without having some ramshackle out-building get in it."

—From a letter, 1961

"I painted me a self-portrait with a pheasant cock that is really a cutter but Regina keeps saying, I think you would look so much better if you had on a tie."

—From a letter, 1953

"My round uncle has brought all his beloved Things home. . . . We have come into the front-porch rockers from there so our front porch now looks like the entrance to an old ladies' rest home. I hadn't rocked for years but I think I am going to excel at it with a little more practice."

—From a letter, 1957

"The cows were grazing on two pale green pastures across the road and behind them, fencing them in, was a black wall of trees with a sharp sawtooth edge that held off the indifferent sky. The pastures were enough to calm her. When she looked out any window in her house, she saw the reflection of her own character."

—*"Greenleaf"*

The unoccupied
tenant-farmer's house in
the barnyard at Andalusia.
Children playing on the
porch had fortuitously
arranged this scene,
symbolic of the rural
people of this area, the
subjects of O'Connor's
fiction.

Edgar Lee Masters

> ❝ *Petersburg is my heart's home. There*
> *I knew at first earth's sun and air;*
> *Still I can see the hills around it,*
> *The people that walked its business square.* ❞
>
> —*"Petersburg"*

The war is still going on—the war between Petersburg and Lewistown, that is. Edgar Lee Masters started it in 1915 when he wrote his *Spoon River Anthology*. People in Lewistown, Illinois, say that he favored neighboring Petersburg by making the characters he drew from there more likable than those who were obviously from Lewistown. Petersburg loves Masters and has preserved his early childhood home there, but Lewistown, where the writer's family moved when he was eleven, would like to forget him. The inhabitants of both towns admit that neither has changed essentially since Masters' day.

I spent some time roaming around this historic Sangamon River region in southern Illinois, which is rich in the lore of Abraham Lincoln. The frontier town of New Salem, where Lincoln lived before going to the legislature of Springfield, is only two miles down the road from Petersburg. When the railroad was built, Lincoln himself surveyed the site of the new town of Petersburg and, later, often came to try cases at the courthouse there. Edgar Lee Masters' poet's ear was tuned by the stories and myths that abounded, and early in life he learned to appreciate the value of individuality, which he later celebrated in *Spoon River Anthology.*

"Petersburg is my heart's home," wrote Masters. His grandparents' farm

Photo of Edgar Lee Masters courtesy Edgar Lee Masters Memorial Home.

was a few miles from town and it was the time spent there that was best remembered. His "own home very early . . . seemed a poor and barren place compared with the house of my grandparents," Masters wrote in his autobiography.

Masters' beloved grandfather, who was immortalized in *Spoon River Anthology* as Davis Matlock, knew that his son and daughter-in-law were shiftless parents and purchased a small house in Petersburg for the young family. Masters wrote later, "Altogether I was not happy in this house that Grandfather gave us, though we lived here in

plenty. From the farm Grandfather sent us loads of potatoes and turnips, of apples, of fuel wood, of everything."

Many years later Edgar Lee Masters recalled a visit his mother made to see him when he was a prosperous lawyer in Chicago. They had many long talks and "went over the whole past of Lewistown and Petersburg, bringing up characters and events that had passed from my mind. . . . The psychological experience of this was truly wonderful. Finally, on the morning she was leaving for Springfield we had a last and rather sobering talk. . . . After putting her on the train . . . I went to my room and immediately wrote 'The Hill' and two or three of the portraits of *Spoon River Anthology*. Almost at once the idea came to me . . . Why not put side by side the stories of two characters interlocked in fate, thus giving both misunderstood souls a chance to be justly weighed?" This was the beginning of Masters' poetic drama, a chronicle of several generations which, when completed, included two hundred and forty-four characters. And thus the war began.

Edgar Lee Masters (1869–1950)—b. Garnett, Kansas.
Major works: *Spoon River Anthology, Vachel Lindsay* (biography), *Across Spoon River* (autobiography).

Edgar Lee Masters Home, corner of Eighth and Jackson Streets, Petersburg, Illinois, open to the public.

From the window of the Masters family home in Petersburg, where he first viewed the world, the author began to store up the tales, experiences, and character sketches of the more than two hundred people, real and imagined, who populate his classic Anthology.

117

A monument in the
Lewistown graveyard
that is similar to
one described in
Spoon River *appears
to be rising in anger
and shaking a fist at
the living world.*

"I sat on the bank above Bernadotte
And dropped crumbs in the water,
Just to see the minnows bump each other,
Until the strongest got the prize.
Or I went to my little pasture
Where the peaceful swine were asleep in the wallow,
Or nosing each other lovingly,
And emptied a basket of yellow corn,
And watched them push and squeal and bite,
And trample each other to get the corn.
And I saw how Christian Dallman's farm,
Of more than three thousand acres,
Swallowed the patch of Felix Schmidt,
As a bass will swallow a minnow.
And I say if there's anything in man—
Spirit, or conscience, or breath of God
That makes him different from fishes or hogs,
I'd like to see it work!"

—Spoon River Anthology

119

Paul Laurence Dunbar

> **" *I write when convenience lets me, or the spirit
> moves me, my object being to do a certain amount
> of work, rather than to work a certain length of
> time. When I first began my career, I wrote
> rapidly, accomplishing without difficulty five
> thousand words a day. Now I write slowly—Oh! so
> slowly. I sometimes spend three weeks on a chapter
> and then am not satisfied with the result. Indeed, I
> have never yet suceeded in perfectly reproducing
> what was in my mind.* "**

—*Quoted in Benjamin Brawley's*
Paul Laurence Dunbar: Poet of His People

*Painting of Paul Laurence Dunbar
courtesy Ohio Historical Society.*

Paul Laurence Dunbar was a tragic figure. He spent most of his brief life in physical and emotional pain, although he achieved considerable success at an early age. The son of former slaves first distinguished himself as a poet in high school and as editor of the school newspaper. His talent was recognized by a group of prominent citizens of his hometown, Dayton, Ohio, and they published his first book of verse, *Oak and Ivy.* Three years later his *Majors and Minors* caught the eye of literary critic William Dean Howells, whose praise in *Harper's Weekly* caused Dunbar to become a national celebrity.

With fame came a demanding schedule of public readings here and abroad, a prestigious job at the Library of Congress, and an ill-fated marriage. He was continually bedeviled by publishers who wanted him to continue using Negro dialect when he preferred to be recognized simply as an American writer. Suddenly, Dunbar was stricken by tuberculosis. His search for a cure in Colorado proved hopeless and he returned to his mother's home in Dayton to die at the age of thirty-four.

The house is a substantial eight-room brick structure on a quiet, tree-shaded street, yet an air of melancholy still pervades its rooms. It is not easy to forget the devoted mother who took in laundry to support herself and to preserve her son's memory in the house he bought for her during his brush with fame.

Dunbar worked prodigiously during his last four years here, in his second-floor study at the front of the house, which he called his "Loafin' Holt." The small daybed is a reminder of the writer's frail health, but there are signs of happier days too: stacks of sheet music for which Dunbar wrote the lyrics, his diploma from Dayton High School, a collection of pipes and beaded Indian moccasins, family photographs, and the top hat and suit he wore to Theodore Roosevelt's inauguration.

Paul Laurence Dunbar
(1872–1906)—b. Dayton, Ohio.
Major works: Poems: *Major and Minors, Lyrics of Lowly Life, Lyrics of the Hearthside, Lyrics of Love and Laughter, Lyrics of Sunshine and Shadow.* Novels: *The Uncalled, The Sport of the Gods.*

Dunbar House State Memorial, 219 North Summit Street, Dayton, Ohio, open to the public.

Mrs. Matilda Dunbar, the author's mother, lived on in their Dayton, Ohio, home for thirty years after his death, carefully preserving his possessions just as he had left them.

Over one of the bookcases hang photographs of the two most influential people in Dunbar's life—his mother, a former slave, and his patron and benefactor, Dr. H. A. Tobey. The bow and swords were collected on his travels.

Part of Dunbar's extensive library (right) is preserved in his "Loafin' Holt," along with souvenirs from trips abroad, photographs, and Indian artifacts from his health-seeking visits to Colorado.

Willa Cather

> *"She gave herself up to the feeling of being at home. It went all through her, that feeling, like getting into a warm bath when one is tired. She was safe from everything, was where she wanted to be, where she ought to be. A plant that has been washed out by a rain storm feels like that, when a kind gardener puts it gently back into its own earth with its own group."*
>
> —The Best Years

Actors trembled when they played Lincoln, Nebraska, so discriminating was the local newspaper's drama critic. Her name was Willa Cather.

After many years as a journalist and editor, she dedicated herself to writing novels and stories, often recalling her childhood on the Nebraska prairie.

The Cather family had moved to Red Cloud, Nebraska, from Virginia in 1883, when Willa was nine years old. Although she spent a scant seven years in the small frontier town, her impressions of that time were vividly invoked later in her work.

When I visited the Cather house with its fourteen-foot ceilings and its rambling succession of rooms, it seemed spacious by present-day standards, but to Willa Cather, who lived there with her six brothers and sisters, her parents and her grandmother, it seemed cramped and small. As the eldest, Willa was given her own room, a corner of the attic partitioned off from the boys' row of beds under the eaves, which she herself papered with a rose-patterned wallpaper bought with the earnings from her first job at Dr. Cook's pharmacy. While Willa

Photo of Willa Cather courtesy Nebraska State Historical Society.

was away at college the room was kept locked.

The town of Red Cloud has diminished since Cather lived there. Still the center of an agricultural district, it has a timeless quality. A walk down Webster Street, the town's main commercial street, reveals several large native brick buildings built in the 1880s, including the Opera House, where William Jennings Bryan once spoke and where Willa Cather was graduated from high school in 1890. A huge old cottonwood tree nearby, saved from the ax by Cather's letters of protest, is another testimony to the writer's strong feeling for the little town's past.

After Willa Cather left Nebraska to become an editor of a magazine in Pittsburgh, she returned occasionally for brief visits with her family. Years later, she claimed that her writing was best when she stopped trying to write and began to remember.

Willa Cather (1873–1947)—b. near Winchester, Virginia. **Major works:** *O Pioneers!, The Song of the Lark, My Ántonia, One of Ours* (1923 Pulitzer Prize), *A Lost Lady, Death Comes for the Archbishop, Shadows on the Rock.*

Willa Cather Pioneer Memorial Museum, Webster Street, Red Cloud, Nebraska, open to the public.
Willa Cather Childhood Home, Third and Cedar Streets, by appointment only.

"There was nothing but land: not a country at all, but the material out of which countries are made."

—My Ántonia

The Cather family home in Red Cloud.

"Their upstairs was a long attic which ran the whole length of the house, from the front door downstairs to the kitchen at the back. Its great charm was that it was unlined. No plaster, no beaver-board lining; just the roof shingles, supported by long, unplaned, splintery rafters that sloped from the roof-peak down to the floor of the attic."

—The Best Years

It is said that Willa changed the date of her birth in the family Bible to make herself seem precocious.

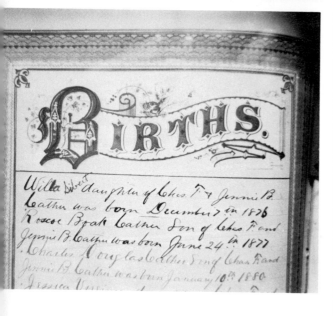

"I remember how the world looked from our sitting-room window as I dressed behind the stove that morning: the low sky was like a sheet of metal; the blonde cornfields had faded out into ghostliness at last."

—My Ántonia

126

"And Lesley's room, when you got there, was very like a snug wooden box."

—The Best Years

"The front hall was dark and cold. The hatrack was hung with an astonishing number of children's hats, caps and cloaks."

—The Song of the Lark

"On Saturdays the children were allowed to go down to the depot to see Seventeen come in. It was a fine sight on winter nights. Sometimes the great locomotive used to sweep in armoured in ice and snow, breathing fire like a dragon, its great red eye shooting a blinding beam along the white road-bed and shining wet rails."

—The Best Years

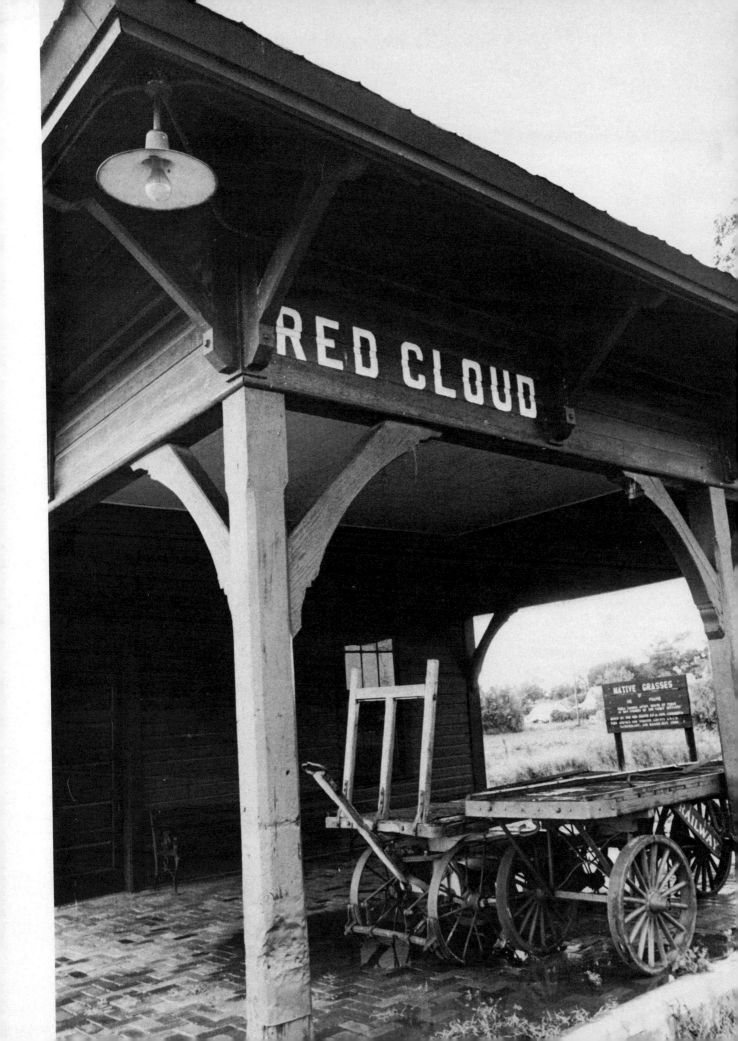

Sinclair Lewis

" *A square smug brown house, rather damp. A narrow concrete walk up to it . . . pillars of thin painted pine surmounted by scrolls and brackets and bumps of jigsawed wood. No shrubbery to shut off the public gaze. A lugubrious bay-window to the right of the porch. Window curtains of starched cheap lace revealing a pink marble table with a conch shell and a Family Bible.* "

—Main Street

Sinclair Lewis did Sauk Centre, Minnesota, a favor. Although residents were initially horrified by the way he depicted the town in *Main Street*, they soon realized that the writer's fame could become a local asset. Lewis is now a year-round preoccupation there, for the town proudly calls itself "Main Street U.S.A., a living museum of an American institution: the Small Town."

The diffident Sinclair Lewis would be aghast to see how he is treasured today by his hometown on the edge of the Minnesota prairie, for he was not kind to it in *Main Street* and called it "Gopher Prairie." His unhappy boyhood must have shaped his view: Dr. E. J. Lewis, the writer's father, was a stern taskmaster whose impossibly high standards gave the younger Lewis a constant sense of failure. "There was no dignity in it nor any hope of greatness. . . . It was not a place to live in, not possibly, not conceivably." After Sinclair Lewis left Sauk Centre to go east to Yale, he lived the rest of his life on the East Coast and in Europe and did not return often to visit. At the end of his life his request to be buried in Sauk Centre surprised everyone.

Sinclair Lewis.

The Lewis house is an easy walk down what is now Sinclair Lewis Avenue away from the Main Street business district. The simple gray clapboard structure is the very model of a small-town doctor's house, equipped with the newest household conveniences such as the first steam-heating pipes in town, a handy pass-through between the dining room and kitchen, and one of the earliest radios, a gift from Sinclair Lewis to his father. Lace-curtained windows and the clutter of too much furniture make the interior of the house dark and oppressive, and I was glad to finish my work there and move outdoors.

I walked back to Main Street past John's Café, a dimly lighted combined lunch counter and recreational center, and the substantial turn-of-the-century Palmer House hotel, both remnants of the bygone era immortalized by the town's favorite son.

In depicting his boyhood home Sinclair Lewis led the revolt of Americans against the genteel Anglican tradition of writing and used the rejection of small-town life as material for what Malcolm Cowley called "a new literature that was as broad and native as the prairies." Lewis was the first American to win the Nobel Prize (1930).

Sinclair Lewis (1885–1951)—b. Sauk Centre, Minnesota.
Major works: *Main Street, Babbitt, Arrowsmith, Elmer Gantry, Dodsworth, Cass Timberlane, It Can't Happen Here.*

Sinclair Lewis Boyhood Home, West Sinclair Lewis Avenue, Sauk Centre, Minnesota, open to the public.

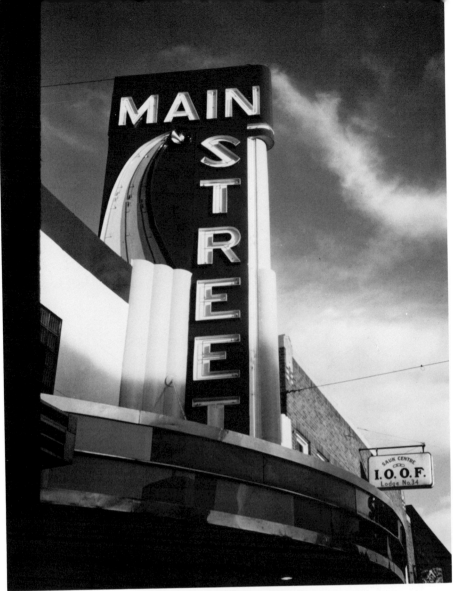

"She saw them playing pool in the stinking room behind Del Snafflin's barber shop, and shaking dice in 'The Smoke House,' and gathered in a snickering knot to listen to the 'juicy stories' of Bert Tybee.... She heard them smacking moist lips over every love scene at the Rosebud Movie Palace."

—Main Street

"She saw that Gopher Prairie was merely an enlargement of all the hamlets they had been passing. . . . The huddled low wooden houses broke the plains scarcely more than would a hazel thicket. The fields swept up to it, past it. It was unprotected and unprotecting."

"In the hallway and front parlor she was conscious of dinginess and lugubriousness and airlessness, but she insisted, 'I'll make it all jolly.' "

—Main Street

Sinclair Lewis' father looks down from the wall of his study. The old radio, one of the earliest made, was a present from the author on publication of Main Street, a touching reminder of Lewis' difficult relationship with his parent.

The Lewis home in Sauk Centre, considered a showplace at the turn of the century when the writer's family lived there, is now restored and proudly hailed as the boyhood home of America's first recipient of the Nobel Prize for Literature.

Dr. Lewis' house was the first in town with modern conveniences, such as this window between kitchen and dining room.

Frank Waters

"In spring too the valley is beautiful and blue, but the beauty is muted and the blue diminished by the intense white light of the steadily rising sun. The mountain walls shrink back. The valley lifts. It is only one amphitheater of many in a vast continental plateau. . . . Occasional clouds of apricot, peach and wild plum blossom soften the harshness in the river bottom below. They repeat the variolithic white splotches of snow and ice and sleet in the cañons above. Both are ephemeral white shadows on the face of the dark enduring earth."

—People of the Valley

I made a pilgrimage to Arroyo Seco, near Taos, New Mexico, to meet Frank Waters. Throughout the West he is a revered literary figure, and I approached his adobe house near the Taos pueblo in the Sangre de Cristo mountains eagerly. As I entered the walled patio I found the writer at his worktable, with his back to the large picture window and its splendid view of aspens and mountains.

Waters' chief interest has been the culture and spiritual life of the Indians of the Southwest, their "pride, dignity, and wild nobility." He believes that indigenous people everywhere are instinctively attuned to their own land and that Anglo-Europeans have much to learn from the Native American's values and idioms. Living with the land is a theme that runs through Frank Waters' work, and he finds our recent awakening to environmental issues interesting. Could his books have contributed to this? He likes to think so.

Waters' house is filled with Indian artifacts. There are Navaho rugs on the floors, a shield cover on the ceiling, a drum in the corner, a score of kachina dolls on a shelf, and feathers in every room, bunched in pottery jars or strung on a willow branch over the door. "Feathers are important to me," said Waters. "The Indians call them the 'breath of life.' "

The writer's workroom is also his bedroom in this cozy one-story house. In a corner is a typical cone-shaped fireplace. Several photographs of friends, such as Mable Dodge Luhan (patroness of Taos artists and writers, including D. H. Lawrence and Georgia O'Keeffe) and her Indian husband, Tony, hang on one wall. On another wall is the hand-painted deerskin tapestry sent to Waters by students in a course on his work at the University of Nevada. His large writing table holds an orderly clutter of pipes and tobacco, penknife and pencil tray; behind the desk is a five-foot-long time-line chart tracing the history of mankind, without which, Waters jokingly said, he couldn't function. It is a fitting reference for the writer who in the course of his work has become an anthropological authority on the early cultures of this continent.

Frank Waters (1902–   )—b. Colorado Springs, Colorado. **Major works:** *People of the Valley, The Man Who Killed the Deer, Masked Gods, Book of the Hopi, Pumpkin Seed Point, Pike's Peak: A Family Saga, Mexico Mystique.*

He lives near Taos, New Mexico.

"Home! How wild and beautiful it was! A thick-walled adobe set back of a stream in a lawn surrounded by great cottonwoods and flanked by a grove of aspens. Behind it a long hay rack and an adobe barn for my three horses."

—Pumpkin Seed Point

The writer's living room contains many artifacts from his extensive collection of Indian art. He explains that the prayer feathers over the doorway—Hopi pahos—are made of small eagle feathers by priests in the kiva during the night of the winter Soyal ceremony. The deerskin (right) was inscribed for Waters by Nevada University students who studied his work. (Opposite, top) Hopi kachina dolls are massed in one corner of Frank Waters' sun-filled bedroom, where he works.

Robinson Jeffers

❝*We have builded us a little house on the sea-cliff here; it is just a year since we came to live in it. A delightful place we think, cormorants on the sea-rocks in front of us, and pelicans drifting overhead; it is a promontory, with water on three sides of us. The house and garage walls are gray granite—sea-boulders, like the natural outcrop of the hill. In foolish frankness, it is the most beautiful place I have ever seen.*❞

—From a letter, 1920

Snapshot of Robinson Jeffers and Edna St. Vincent Millay at Tor House, 1930s; photographer unknown.

This poet built his house of enormous stones hauled from the beach below. And when Robinson Jeffers discovered it was a healthful form of exercise and a complement to his sedentary hours spent writing, he continued his stonework as a daily ritual, adding rooms here, a garage there, for the rest of his life. "My fingers had the art to make stone love stone," Jeffers wrote in his poem "Tor House."

Tor House, on the spectacular California coast at Carmel, seems to reflect a particular love of the British Isles; the Hawk Tower, for example, could easily be a medieval cairn from Ireland. But Tor House has many cultural layers. Cemented in the walls are red stones from the Great Wall of China, pieces of marble recovered from the San Francisco earthquake, a stone from the pyramid of Cheops, and some pre-Columbian carvings, gifts from traveling friends.

Everything at Tor House has a history. I noticed a number of abalone shells around the garden and discovered that they were remnants of an ancient Indian feeding ground or fishing place. Robinson Jeffers' desk was made from the timbers of an old mission nearby.

Mornings, for Jeffers, were devoted to writing. The poet would retire to an attic room to work until his wife, Una, called the family to lunch. Building and gardening were saved for the afternoons. The Jefferses'

shared passion for poetry, beauty, and family life are manifested everywhere at Tor House, the private world they created here on the edge of the sea.

Robinson Jeffers (1887–1962)—b. Pittsburgh, Pennsylvania.
Major works: *Roan Stallion, Tamar, and Other Poems, The Women at Point Sur, Cawdor and Other Poems, Dear Judas and Other Poems, Give Your Heart to the Hawks, Selected Poetry.*

Tor House, 26304 Ocean View Avenue, Carmel, California, open by appointment only.

A view of Tor House from the top of the Hawk Tower, which Jeffers named for the hawk that swooped down and perched on the structure as he built it.

Memorable stones, including this gravestone for one of the family pets, are everywhere at Tor House.

"I spend a couple of hours nearly every afternoon at stone-masonry, having still much to build about the place; or bringing up stone from the beach, violent exercise; and physically I'm harder than at any time," Jeffers wrote to a friend. This view of the coast is from the Hawk Tower.

A porthole from the ship that carried Napoleon from Elba was found on the beach by Jeffers. Many times through the years, the window—which normally needs a wrench to open it—has been found mysteriously ajar. Jeffers' desk and chair, originally in the attic of Tor House, now rest in the ground floor room of the Hawk Tower. Nearby is the tower's cornerstone.

RJ
SUIS MANIBUS ME
TURREM FALCONIS
FECIT MCMXXIV

Henry Miller

> **"** *The last time it happened was while I was writing* Plexus. *During the year or so that I was occupied with this work . . . the inundation was almost continuous. Huge blocks—particularly the dream parts—came to me just as they appear in print and without any effort on my part, except that of equating my own rhythm with that of the mysterious dictator who had me in his thrall. . . . Bang! Like a sack of coal it would spill out. I could keep it up for three or four hours at a stretch, interrupted only by the arrival of the mailman.* **"**

—Big Sur and the Oranges of Hieronymus Bosch

*I*gnored the sign on the door. He didn't mean a word of it. Henry Miller was still a garrulous, lovable genius, though now he was more raconteur and sage than hellion.

Miller's yeasty celebration of life began in the Yorkville area of New York City, but the family eventually moved to Brooklyn, and it is those years between the ages of five and ten the writer recalled as his paradise. "I remember the names of the boys and the young men who were older than me—they were my heroes! I remember them still, all of them." Miller associates his free spirit with those early days on the streets of Brooklyn. He kept a trace of a Brooklyn accent.

When Henry Miller went to live in Paris in the 1930s and published his first work, *Tropic of Cancer*, the book caused a furor for its explicit sexual language and freewheeling prose. It was banned in the United States, although, as smuggled copies came in and influenced writers at home, it marked the end of post-Victorian literary inhibitions in America. Lawrence Durrell said of his friend, "American literature begins and ends with the meaning of what Miller has done."

Henry Miller's unremarkable white, two-storied Georgian house in suburban Los Angeles was a visual feast, a joyful array of posters, photographs, his watercolor paintings, tapestries, and souvenirs. It was no surprise for me to see that his house showed the same quality of exuberance as its owner. I had just seen a fine exhibit of his paintings at a gallery near his old home in Big Sur, and was interested to see that painting was as important to him as his writing. "Painting is connected with joy and pleasure. Writing is not always that. I try to make it that, but there's a different kind of work involved." He did both, freely and intuitively, all his life.

The largest room in Henry Miller's house was where he painted, and it was also the center of house-hold activities, with an open kitchen at one side, sliding glass doors leading out to a patio and pool, and a large Ping-Pong table crowded with paints, brushes, and recent work.

To write, Miller moved to a desk in his bedroom, surrounded by more posters and photographs of family and friends. Love keeps us young, I thought when the writer who had been married five times showed me a picture of his current romantic interest. "Oh, love is very important. I do think so. Love and my work, which I don't think of as work, you know. I consider it play."

Henry Miller (1891–1980)—b. New York City, New York.
Major works: *Tropic of Cancer, Tropic of Capricorn, The Cosmological Eye, The Colossus of Maroussi, Sexus, Plexus, Nexus, Big Sur and the Oranges of Hieronymus Bosch, The Books in My Life.*

He lived in Pacific Palisades, California. His house is not open to the public.

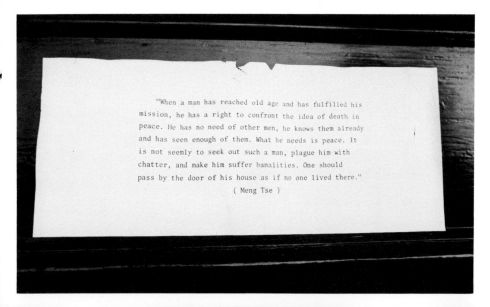

"When a man has reached old age and has fulfilled his
mission, he has a right to confront the idea of death in
peace. He has no need of other men, he knows them already
and has seen enough of them. What he needs is peace. It
is not seemly to seek out such a man, plague him with
chatter, and make him suffer banalities. One should
pass by the door of his house as if no one lived there."

(Meng Tse)

Describing his decorations, Miller pointed to
a living-room wall. "This tapestry was done
in France from one of my works. I could
have more, but I don't know where I would
hang them. This house is so full of things
on the walls. Even the ceiling, as you can
see." The life-size figures carved of wood
were made by an admirer of Miller's work
and simply left on his doorstep.

The writer concedes: "This bathroom has become well-known. When people come to the house the first thing they say is, 'Where is your bathroom?'"

Anaïs Nin

❝ *The house gives me peace and beauty. The swimming restores me. I sit at my desk at seven-thirty. I work until lunchtime. At four I go to the post office. There I face an avalanche of letters, manuscripts, books from publishers. . . . I have to return manuscripts unread. I answer letters with a card. Correspondence with colleges where I have to send posters, photographs, announcements before lectures. And I must edit all the Diaries because no one else can do it.* **❞**

—The Diary of Anaïs Nin, Vol. VII

I believe one writes because one has to create a world in which one can live. . . . I had to create a world of my own, like a climate, a country, an atmosphere in which I could breathe, reign," Anaïs Nin wrote in her diary.

Nin's house is like her diaries, richly personal, evocative of the woman herself. Designed in 1959 by architect Frank Lloyd Wright's son, Lloyd Wright, the one-level house is built of natural materials and sits high on a hill overlooking Los Angeles' Silver Lake. The structure is one with the landscape, an environment of delicate colors—pinks, lavender, and watery blues—and of serenity and calm.

Anaïs Nin's friend Kozuko Sugisaki, here from Japan to translate Nin's diaries into Japanese, escorted me through the house with the late writer's poodle, Piccolino, following close at our heels. She led me through sliding glass doors to the terrace with its fabulous view of the city below, partly obscured by haze that day, and the emerald-green swimming pool—where the writer used to take a daily swim—bordered at intervals by rocks and low shrubs arranged in the Japanese manner. Placed near the pool's

Anaïs Nin's portrait by Renate Druks.

edge, almost hidden by a tuft of grass, was a tiny spirit house that Nin brought back from Indonesia. At the far end of the pool was the teahouse, a replica of those found in private Japanese gardens, where Kozuko had arranged a simple floral tribute to Nin, who died in 1977.

With Piccolino still at my heels, I found Anaïs Nin's small, book-filled study, which occupies one of the four corners of the house, its high windows allowing only a treetop view of the back garden. Her dainty portable typewriter rests on the desk top,

which extends the length of one wall, and nearby lies the familiar black leather attaché case, which she carried with her everywhere. A very disciplined writer, Anaïs Nin devoted every morning to her work, rising early to do her most creative writing before ten o'clock. Afternoons were devoted to answering the mountain of letters that arrived at her door every week.

Nin's greatest legacy was undoubtedly her diaries—35,000 handwritten pages recording her development as an artist. In Volume V she wrote, "When I don't write I feel my world shrinking. I feel I am in a prison. I feel I lose my fire, my color. It should be a necesssity, as the sea needs to heave. I call it breathing."

Anaïs Nin (1903–1977)—b. Paris, France.
Major works: *Winter of Artifice, House of Incest, Under a Glass Bell, A Spy in the House of Love, Delta of Venus: Erotica by Anaïs Nin, The Diary of Anaïs Nin.*

She lived in Los Angeles, California. Her house is not open to the public.

Kozuko Sugisaki, who is translating Anaïs Nin's diary into Japanese, appears in the doorway. Los Angeles' Silver Lake district is reflected in the picture window and an Indonesian spirit house from the author's trip to Thailand is placed by the pool.

"At twenty to seven, Piccolino, who lies on the bed, seems heavier, and he wakes me." The author's bedroom is dominated by a huge collage by Jean Varda and opens on to her pool, where she enjoyed a daily swim. The Japanese teahouse, visible in the distance, was acquired by the writer after one of her extensive visits to the Orient and provided her with a haven for solitude and meditation.

*Anaïs Nin's study
contains manuscripts
and original editions
of the voluminous
diary, as well as the
books she printed on
her hand press in
New York City. The
covers were designed
and engraved by her
husband, Ian Hugo.*

Jessamyn West

> **"***Home, when you grow big enough to accept it, is not Bigger Township or Fairmont School, or Pepper Tree House or Los Feliz Boulevard. It is the sand and sky, the sun and stars, the wind and sea of the whole earth we live on; the planet we call 'home.'***"**

—The Life I Really Lived

Adversity can be beneficial; at least it was in Jessamyn West's case. In her early thirties she was bedridden for two years with tuberculosis, and during that time she began to write stories. She had always wanted to be a writer but decided to become a professor of English instead because writing "seemed so great and noble a thing. I thought it was presumptuous—you know, vain." Her husband, Max, persuaded her to submit the stories to magazines, and when they began to be accepted, Jessamyn West finally decided that she was a writer.

One of the habits that she picked up in those days was to write while reclining, and she still is most comfortable working that way. Her work space is in her bedroom and she has arranged a windowed alcove where she can watch the birds feed as she writes, propped up on pillows with a lapboard across her knees. There is a desk in the room but she rarely uses it.

When she needs solitude, she goes to a hideaway in the attic, reached by a narrow, hard-to-find stairway behind a panel in the corner of the bedroom. This retreat consists of two book-lined rooms with a divan in one corner where she can write. It is a place that is hers alone. "When you're downstairs, people can get at you. But they really have to have something important to say to go climbing those stairs!"

Another result of Jessamyn West's bout with serious illness is her exuberant appreciation of life. She is warm and garrulous, full of fun. Ray Bradbury admiringly describes her as "ribald and jolly," and her home in California's Napa Valley reflects this spirit. She and Max moved to this pleasant ranch house forty years ago, when Max became superintendent of schools in Napa. Here on several acres of lovingly landscaped ground are an orchard, a pond, a grape arbor, a swimming pool, a stable for horses, and a Japanese pavilion. The house teems with life—three dogs, three wary cats, and birds in and out of cages. Max describes their wine cellar and smiles approvingly when he reveals that it is now a storage place for manuscripts. To paraphrase from one of her own stories in *The Friendly Persuasion*, Jessamyn West lacks for very little here in the Napa Valley.

Jessamyn West (1902–   )—b. Indiana.

Major works: *Cress Delahanty, The Friendly Persuasion, Love Is Not What You Think, The Quaker Reader, A Matter of Time, Massacre at Fall Creek, The Woman Said Yes, The Life I Really Lived.*

She lives in Napa, California.

Jessamyn West and her mother in an early tintype on the wall of her study, along with a photo of her Quaker grandmother. The cross on the left is fashioned from wedding rings—hers, her sister's, her mother's, and her grandmother's.

(Above) The study where Jessamyn West does most of her writing.

The writer's hideaway in the attic.

Ross Macdonald (Kenneth Millar) & Margaret Millar

> " *A rattle of leaves woke me sometime before dawn. A hot wind was breathing in at the bedroom window. I got up and closed the window and lay in bed and listened to the wind.*
>
> *After a while it died down, and I got up and opened the window again. Cool air, smelling of fresh ocean and slightly used West Los Angeles, poured into the apartment. I went back to bed and slept until I was awakened in the morning by my scrub jays.* "

—The Underground Man

Ross Macdonald's house is going to the dogs. When I drove up to the front door of Kenneth Millar's sprawling ranch-style home, two German shepherds greeted me, along with their sidekick, a medium-sized terrier. The fourth canine, a Newfoundland, joined us later when Margaret Millar brought him home from a walk on the beach.

Margaret and Kenneth Millar—Ross Macdonald is his pen name—have written more than fifty books between them. Margaret began what was to become the family cottage industry by writing her first mystery novel in 1941, and she enjoyed the experience so much that she suggested her husband try his hand at it. Their friend W. H. Auden was teaching at the University of Michigan, where Kenneth Millar was working on his Ph.D., and the Millars credit him with encouraging them in the mystery-writing genre, to which Auden gave considerable literary importance.

Kenneth Millar is a Californian, even though he spent his youth in Canada, and he writes about a California that is a microcosm of our so-ciety, where traditional relationships and values have been transformed by technology, creating a new world of things to which we must learn to adapt. Not surprisingly, the Millars are avid conservationists, active as Sierra Club members and as co-founders of the Santa Barbara Citizens for Environmental Defense. Margaret has recently published a book on the flora of their region.

Both Millars write best with their feet up. Margaret has a favorite chair in her bedroom with a table-like arm, reminiscent of those in schoolrooms. There she retires to write, being careful to close the door behind her to keep out the canine members of the family.

Kenneth is more tolerant of his four-footed friends while working. He allows them to accompany him to his bedroom, where he stretches out in an ancient leather club-chair-cum-ottoman and pulls a board across the arms to write. The dogs know that after a time at work he will put on his wide-brimmed hat and take them outdoors for a romp.

Ross Macdonald (Kenneth Millar) (1915–   )—b. Los Gatos, California.
Major works: *The Wycherly Woman, The Zebra-Striped Hearse, Black Money, Instant Enemy, The Goodbye Look, The Underground Man, Sleeping Beauty, The Blue Hammer.*

Margaret Millar (1915–   )—b. Kitchener, Ontario, Canada.
Major works: *The Invisible Worm, The Weak-Eyed Bat, The Devil Loves Me, Fire Will Freeze, Wives and Lovers, The Birds and the Beasts Were There, Ask for Me Tomorrow, Beast in View.*

They live in Santa Barbara, California.

Kenneth
Millar—Ross
Macdonald—is
considered a thinking
man's mystery writer.
Most of his novels are
built around a
middle-aged detective
hero, Lew Archer,
whose adventures are
created on a lapboard
in a corner of the
author's bedroom.
Margaret also works
in longhand in her
own bedroom. She
was the first Millar to
write a mystery
novel.

Ray Bradbury

" *The city waited twenty thousand years. . . . The city waited with its windows and its black obsidian walls and its sky towers and its unpennanted turrets, with its untrod streets and its untouched doorknobs, with not a scrap of paper or a fingerprint upon it. The city waited while the planet arced in space, following its orbit about a blue-white sun, and the seasons passed from ice to fire and back to ice and then to green fields and yellow summer meadows.* "

—The Illustrated Man

A gorilla greeted me to say, "Ray Bradbury is a working writer. Please don't knock."

Once inside, I found a fun-lover's paradise, where trinkets, toys, drawings, posters, accumulated geegaws, and games overflowed the two rooms of the writer's office in a slightly run-down building high above elegant Wilshire Boulevard in Beverly Hills.

"I hope I never have to move," he says, surveying the clutter. Here, in addition to his many works of fiction, Bradbury has written two plays, several screenplays and television specials, and an opera. He designs futuristic exhibits for Walt Disney Productions and makes sketches for his own book jackets.

Despite the nonchalant appearance of this environment, Bradbury does not have a casual attitude about his work. "You work on seven or eight things at a time because four or five of them are going to collapse," he says. Bradbury lives in a nearby Los Angeles community, but he tries to put in a seven- or eight-hour stint at his office every day. He has no secretary. "I'm such a good typist, I don't have to worry about mistakes. And I want to be alone. Totally alone. The rest of the time I'm very gregarious, as you can tell."

Even though he is fascinated by things mechanical, including a sophisticated electric typewriter, Bradbury does not fly in airplanes and he will not drive a car. Two bicycles lean against the wall. "I have my bikes here for getting around Beverly Hills," said the master of science fiction.

Ray Bradbury (1920–   )—b. Waukegan, Illinois.
Major works: *The Martian Chronicles, The Illustrated Man, Farenheit 451, A Medicine for Melancholy, The Autumn People, Dandelion Wine.*

He lives in Los Angeles, California.

Amid the clutter of memorabilia that spans the history of movies, television, and cartooning, Bradbury works at his profession of spinning fantasy. The stuffed friend is Bullwinkle, a television cartoon favorite of his from the 1960s. The bicycle has a practical use—it is the only vehicle Bradbury is willing to operate himself.

Leaning on a sophisticated electric typewriter, one of his few concessions to the electronic age, the writer surveys his collection. He is also a frustrated actor and keeps a cardboard carton filled with unsold tickets to one of his plays as a reminder "to be humble about the theater."